£5

D0521943

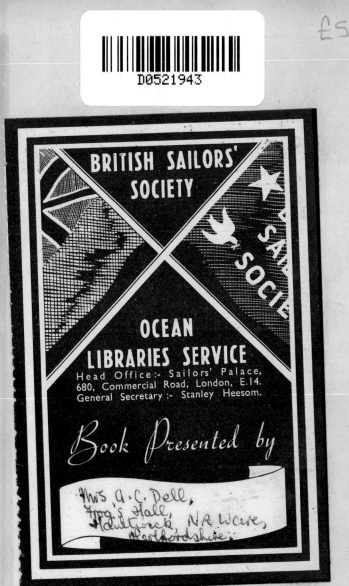

BRITISH SAILORS' SOCIETY

OCEAN LIBRARIES SERVICE

Head Office:- Sailors' Palace,
680, Commercial Road, London, E.14.
General Secretary :- Stanley Heesom.

Book Presented by

Mrs. A. C. Dell,
Frog's Hall,
Hadham, Nr. Ware,
Hertfordshire.

DOWN TO EARTH

The Cox brothers pick up morse messages from Professor Pollenport, who had left the earth five years before and is building a spaceship on Antigeos for his return. The Professor's original flight had been backed by Lord Sanderlake's newspaper, whose science editor he had been. The Coxes apply to Sanderlake for help in contacting the Professor. Sanderlake agrees, hoping for a "scoop", but unscrupulous financiers break into the secret and fantastic plans are made to exploit the planets as colonies. . . .

Books by Paul Capon

—

DOWN TO EARTH

by

PAUL CAPON

WILLIAM HEINEMANN LTD
MELBOURNE :: LONDON :: TORONTO

FIRST PUBLISHED 1954

PRINTED IN GREAT BRITAIN
AT THE WINDMILL PRESS
KINGSWOOD, SURREY

CHAPTER I

I

A COLD wind was streaming across Pengeness Head and a cold grey sea was breaking on its eastern shore, throwing up more shingle on to the vast shingle-banks for which the peninsula is remarkable. The wind rattled the doors and windows of the huts that huddled round the lighthouse, and rippled the stretches of dead water out on the marsh where the water-birds stood with their backs to it, like old men with hunched shoulders and their hands in their pockets. And further inland the wind swept over the abandoned rifle-ranges and wailed into the streets of the peninsula's one town, Brydd, so that it was small wonder there was nobody about that afternoon.

Digby Cox, coasting down Beacon Hill in his ancient station-wagon, surveyed the town from afar and shuddered. "My home-town," he muttered, "and how I hate it. Who could be a success in Brydd?"

Once Brydd had stood as an outpost against possible invasion, but, since the invention of aircraft, those days were past, and now there was little reason for its continued existence. It was on the road to nowhere and it was the centre of nothing. Its monastery had been a ruin for four hundred years, its barracks for forty, and yet three thousand people lingered on, taking in each other's washing and braving the winds that swept in from all four quarters.

Digby came to the foot of the hill and accelerated

angrily. "Bankrupt," he exclaimed, with a certain relish. "That's the long and the short of it, we're bankrupt. Ruined by big ideas and small means!"

The station-wagon rattled over the disused railway's level-crossing, and then Brydd's huge and ugly church loomed into view. Digby skirted it, came out into the Square and pulled up in front of the shop that had been his father's, and was now his and his brother's. It was a fine, double-fronted shop—shuttered today, for early-closing—and its stock mainly consisted of wireless-sets, television-sets and all the accessories that the modern world is heir to. There was even a tape-recorder and, as Digby let himself into the shop, his eye fell on it, and he gave a short laugh. "I must have been crazy when I ordered that," he reflected. "Who on earth in Brydd would want a tape-recorder, even in this year of grace nineteen seventy-three?"

He closed the door hurriedly because of the wind, but some of it was too quick for him and a number of leaflets lying on the counter went leaping into the air and scattered themselves on the floor. He cursed sombrely and went through into the back of the shop.

There was no sign of his brother either in their living-room or in the kitchen, so he had to brave the wind again, crossing the garden towards the large shed at the garden's end that served them as a workshop. Strange-looking aerials festooned the shed, which was a wooden one, and it had been built at that inconvenient distance from the house on the insistence of the insurance company. "One spot of lightning," the agent had said, "and up the whole show will go in smoke! To say nothing of the outlandish voltages you'll be using."

Digby pushed open the door and went in. "Hullo, Bryan," he said, but his brother, at the far end of the

2

shed, had ear-phones on and did not hear him. In any case, he had quite extraordinary powers of concentration.

An electric kettle had just come to the boil on the bench nearest the door, and Digby went to it. He spooned some tea into the tea-pot and poured in the boiling water.

"Hey, Bryan," he shouted. "I'm back and I've made tea!"

Bryan jerked off the ear-phones and swung round. "A most extraordinary thing!" he exclaimed. "I've been analysing sun-spots on a ten-M wave-length, and now I seem to be picking up morse!"

Digby strode the length of the shed and studied the instrument-panel. "Nonsense," he said. "You can't be picking up morse on that fixing. Either your screening is faulty or you're cuckoo—and my preference is for the latter explanation."

"No, seriously," said Bryan, holding up the ear-phones. "You listen."

"No, thanks. Those things give me a headache, and I've enough on my plate without that."

"But you can read morse, and I can't! Come on, Digby—I'll hook up the amplifier!"

"Even that doesn't tempt me," said Digby, shaking his head. "I suppose I'm just not in the mood for cosmic morse. Come and have a cup of tea, and I'll tell you my news, which is lousy."

Bryan reluctantly climbed down from his stool and followed his brother to the bench where the tea-pot stood. "You mean we're out of business?" he asked.

"As good as. My efforts to negotiate an overdraft were turned aside with a light laugh, so then there was nothing for it except to go to Cunningham and tell him we couldn't meet his account. I asked him for another six months' credit, but if he heard me, he didn't let on. In fact, all he could say was, 'Well, Mr. Cox, I'm prepared to help you to the extent of taking back everything that's unsold——' "

Bryan interrupted his brother with a gasp. "All this?" he asked, with a gesture towards the equipment with which the shed was filled.

"Most of it. And half the stock in the shop. Actually, there is just a faint chance that we can pull through, but to do so we shall have to give up all dreams of fame and glory. No more experiments in radaroscopy, no more research into the nature of cosmic rays, and no more fun and games with the universe as our playground. Instead, we shall just have to devote ourselves to repairing radios, selling light-bulbs and installing door-bells, which will be a change, to say least of it."

He poured out two cups of tea, and for some minutes nothing broke the silence except the whine and throb of the generating-plant in the adjoining out-house. Bryan's expression suggested that his heart would break and all Digby's sympathy went out to him. At eighteen, he reflected, one has met with fewer disappointments than at twenty-five, and they are proportionately harder to take. Also, Bryan was the more single-minded of the two and exploring cosmic space by means of radar-techniques was his ruling passion.

"When's Cunningham sending for the stuff?" he asked, at length.

"He mentioned Friday."

"The day after tomorrow? . . . Oh, God!"

He drank his tea and returned to the bench where he had been working."

"Digby, I wish you'd listen to this morse," he murmured. "It's most peculiar."

As he spoke, he inserted the jack-plug of the amplifier

and pressed a couple of switches. The amplifier hissed and crackled and then, underlying the atmospherics, came the unmistakable stutter of morse.

"There you are, Digby!" he shouted. "What's that? Morse or Scotch mist?"

Digby joined him and stood for a few moments listening. "Yes, it's morse, all right," he agreed presently, "but it's as I said. Your screening's faulty and you're picking up morse on another——"

He broke off and the degree of interest in his expression increased. He put his head nearer the amplifier and Bryan asked what had struck him.

Digby made an impatient gesture, then exclaimed, "Good God! . . . Bryan, where's a piece of paper?"

His excitement was infectious, and Bryan hurriedly thrust a note-pad and pencil in his hand. Digby scribbled rapidly and too illegibly for Bryan to be able to make out the message, but under his breath he suddenly muttered, "My God—*Pollenport*!"

The name burst across Bryan's consciousness like a star-shell, and he gazed up into his brother's face in wild surmise. Was he really getting a message from Jonah Pollenport, the man who, five years before, had commanded the first spaceship ever to leave the earth?

As long as Digby scribbled there was nothing for Bryan to do except curb his impatience, and half a millennium seemed to creep by before at last his brother said, "All right, Bryan. You can switch off."

"But the morse is still coming through!"

"Yes, I know, but it's simply the same message repeating itself on an endless band," said Digby, then added, with maddening calm, "As a matter of fact, it's from Jonah Pollenport, and he's on the planet Antigeos."

"Well, for God's sake tell me what the message is before I burst!" cried Bryan, switching off.

5

Digby consulted his note, and read, "This is Jonah Pollenport calling the Earth from the planet Antigeos. Will anyone receiving this signal please acknowledge on the same wave-length. The signal will now be repeated. . . .' "

"Antigeos?" whispered Bryan. "Then it does exist after all?"

"Presumably," said the calmer Digby. "Unless—unless we're the victims of a hoax."

Bryan hardly heard him. He was gazing at the silent amplifier rather as Sir Galahad must have gazed at the Holy Grail and, when he found his voice, he asked what were the chances of anyone else picking up the signal.

"Small," Digby assured him. "We haven't a monopoly of the ultra-short waves, but we do know that there isn't a great deal of research being done in that field. Of course, Pollenport may be using a variety of wave-lengths, but, even if he is, he's limited to the ultra-short ones by the Heaviside–Kennelly layer."

"Naturally," said Bryan. "So now we just build an enormously powerful transmitter and make contact with him?"

"Oh yes? And how can we build an enormously powerful transmitter between now and Friday? And, without cash or credit, where are we going to get the necessary equipment for stepping up our voltages from?"

"From Cunningham!" cried Bryan. "Yes, we'll have to let him into the secret. It's horrible having to share the glory with him, but there's nothing else for it."

Digby laughed. "You're quite an optimist, aren't you?" he murmured. "Brother, you can take it from me that Mr. Cunningham isn't interested in glory. He wouldn't see any percentage in it, and the knowledge

6

that we've picked up a message from Pollenport would leave him as cold as an iceberg. No, we've got to think of something else."

He strolled pensively back to the tea-pot and poured himself out another cup of tea. He lit a cigarette with shaking hands and Bryan switched on the amplifier once more. The morse was still stuttering faintly behind the atmospherics and Bryan's sense of frustration became almost impossible to bear. "Think of it, Digby!" he murmured. "You and I are the first men on Earth to get *proof* of the existence of Antigeos!"

Digby didn't reply, and Bryan struggled to recall all that he'd ever heard about Antigeos. To the best of his knowledge the planet's existence had originally been hypothetised by a Professor Wittenhagen as early as the nineteen-forties, but it wasn't until nearly twenty years later that Wittenhagen's theory had been published. According to the theory, Antigeos constituted the Solar System's tenth planet, and that it had escaped the astronomers' notice for so long was accounted for by the fact that it shared the Earth's orbit, revolving round the sun at the same speed as the Earth and at a point diametrically opposite to it, so that, from the terrestrial point of view, it was for ever hidden by the glare of the sun itself.

As regards details of the Pollenport Expedition, Bryan was hazy He had been only thirteen at the time, and he was about to question his brother when Digby suddenly spoke.

"I've got it!" he exclaimed. "Lord Sanderlake!"

"Sanderlake?" echoed Bryan. "But why him in particular?"

In fact, he found Digby's suggestion puzzling. He only knew Lord Sanderlake as the proprietor of the *Daily Messenger*, and he instinctively felt that it would be a mistake to hand over their secret to the popular Press. If they did that, the whole thing would probably be taken out of their hands and all they'd get out of it was a miserable cheque for a hundred or so.

"Well, I suggest Sanderlake," said Digby, "because he was the original instigator of the Pollenport Expedition. Didn't you know that?"

Bryan shook his head. "No, I didn't. Tell me about it."

"Well, Jonah Pollenport, you know, was the *Daily Messenger* science editor, and I forget just how it was that he got hold of the Antigeos theory, but anyway he did get hold of it and then Sanderlake took it up in a big way. He financed the building of the spaceship, and the idea was that Pollenport should circumastrogate the orbit to find out whether or not Antigeos existed. There were any number of snags and hitches, but in due course the spaceship did take off—and has never been heard of since!"

"And it was never intended that he should land on Antigeos?" Brian put in.

"Definitely not, because of the difficulty of taking off again. No, I can only suppose that Pollenport is on Antigeos because he crashed on it, and presumably he and his companions have spent the last five years in building a transmitter out of parts of the wrecked spaceship."

"Who were his companions?"

"Let me see—I think he took about four people with him. A chap called Sam Spencross was one and he was an expert on reaction-propulsion. And then there was Pollenport's assistant, whose name I forget—I think he was a negro, and another young man who bought his passage by winning a football pool."

"Oh yes, I remember," said Bryan. "I remember that

8

at school we were all sick with envy of him. Wasn't his name Timothy something? Fox, or Fry? Anyway, a Quaker name."

"Penn," said Digby. "Yes, that's it—Timothy Penn. And I think that's about the lot, but it was strongly rumoured at the time that Pollenport's daughter had managed to get on board as a stowaway. The rumour was never confirmed, but she certainly disappeared at about that time."

"And now you think we ought to get in touch with Sanderlake?" murmured Bryan. "But if we do that, won't he just pinch our secret and then tell us to get lost?"

"No, I don't think that that would be quite Sanderlake's style," said Digby. "He's a bit of a crook, of course, but not a petty one, and in any case there's no need for us to tell him the wave-length. Come on, let's go and telephone him!"

II

Lord Sanderlake was rather frightened of storms, except for those of his own making, and as he listened to the wind howling around the turrets of Narraway Towers he bitterly regretted his decision to winter in England. Squall upon squall of rain rattled among the trees outside and he visibly shuddered, cowering deeper into his armchair and biting his finger-nails nervously. In fact, he was an excessively timid man and the struggle he put up against his timidity had been the main-spring of his whole enormously successful career. He ranted and blustered, pretended to be Napoleon and got his own way, but underneath it all he was still little Jim

Cooper, who was afraid of storms, pussy-cats, the dark and his own shadow.

The red telephone at his side buzzed discreetly and, reaching for it, he grunted into the mouthpiece.

A woman's voice answered him. "Lord Sanderlake?"

He recognised the voice as that of his senior secretary and grunted again. She was speaking from the *Daily Messenger* offices, to which the telephone was connected by private line, and Lord Sanderlake heard her say something about a young man who wanted to speak to him.

"Can't hear a thing," he snapped. "Speak up, Dora—there's a storm here making more noise than the wrath of God. A terrible storm!"

So Dora spoke up and told him she had a young man called Digby Cox on the line. "He's speaking from Brydd," she said, "and he refuses to talk to anyone except you. He's a very insistent young man and he assures me he's on to the greatest news-story since—since——" She broke off and tittered, causing Lord Sanderlake to writhe with fury.

"Don't titter, Dora," he roared. "Since what?"

"Well, since James Watt invented the steam-engine," she told him. "I informed Mr. Cox you were down in the country and he asked for your number. Am I to give it to him?"

"Yes," said Lord Sanderlake, and hung up. He had once missed a scoop through refusing to take a telephone-call, and he had no intention of allowing it to happen again.

A sudden appalling crash brought him out of his chair with a jerk and he gazed fearfully towards the windows. Then he touched the bell and, going to the tantalus, poured himself out a stiff whisky.

The butler came in as he was drinking the whisky

and, in the nick of time, Lord Sanderlake assumed one of his several great-man poses. "Oh, Davidson," he said, "I think a chimney-pot or something's been blown down. Go and investigate, will you?"

Davidson was a bulky, saturnine man, youngish for a butler, and his dark eyes, as he gazed at his master, were inimical.

"Certainly, my lord. I'll send——"

"You'll send no one!" exclaimed Lord Sanderlake, practically shouting because he was also afraid of butlers. "You'll go yourself, and find out exactly what's happened. Good God, man, you're not scared of a little wind, are you?"

"No, my lord; but I must respectfully point out that it is not my place——"

"Your place!" snorted Lord Sanderlake. "Your place is to do what I tell you and like it! You've been reading too much Compton-Burnett, that's your trouble."

"I do read Miss Compton-Burnett," admitted the butler, conversationally, "but I trust I am not so protean as to allow myself to be influenced by that lady's works, admirable though they are. No, my lord, it's simply a matter of——"

He was interrupted by the telephone ringing—the black one this time—and Lord Sanderlake grabbed it. "For God's sake, Davidson," he muttered, with his hand over the receiver, "find out about that chimney-pot and don't talk so much. . . . Hullo?"

His caller announced himself as Digby Cox and lost no time in stating his business. "Well, Lord Sanderlake, my brother and I have some very important news for you," he said, "and we're wondering if we could come and see you."

"News? What news?"

"I'd prefer to let it wait till we meet."

11

"No, no, no. I can't hold myself at the mercy of every crank and crackpot in——"

"All right, Lord Sanderlake. We simply thought you'd be interested, that's all. Particularly since we're on to the biggest news-break since——"

"I know. Since Watt invented the steam-engine."

"Well, actually I was going to say since Columbus reported back from America."

"Oh, so you've raised the ante, have you? But surely, young man, you can give me an inkling, just a hint as to what it's all about?"

There was a long pause, then Digby Cox said: "It's about Jonah Pollenport. You see, we've had a message from him."

Lord Sanderlake gasped. "What's that? From Jonah Pollenport? Then where the hell is he?"

"May we come and see you?"

"What? Yes, of course." Lord Sanderlake was almost stammering in his excitement. "You're at Brydd, aren't you? Well, I'll send a car for you."

"We've got a car, thank you," said Digby, "and we'll be with you within the hour."

Lord Sanderlake's hand was shaking so badly that he could hardly replace the receiver on the cradle. "Jonah Pollenport!" he muttered, and finished his whisky. "Why, if that young man's speaking the truth Watt and Columbus just aren't in the running! If that doesn't lift us to the ten-million mark, nothing will."

He forgot all about the storm and, dropping into an armchair, sat gazing into a future that shimmered with golden promise. For five years he had been guiltily conscious of mishandling the Pollenport business, and now it looked as if he might be given a chance to redeem himself. Or was someone trying to take him for a ride?

His thoughts were interrupted by Davidson returning

and announcing that it wasn't a chimney-pot after all. "It was an elm, my lord," he said. "Or, rather, the branch of an elm."

Lord Sanderlake's nervousness revived and he moistened his lips. "Yes? What happened?"

"The branch came down on the small conservatory, virtually demolishing it," said Davidson. "To be frank, my lord, I have often questioned the advisability of allowing such treacherous trees to flourish in the vicinity of the house. As your lordship no doubt knows, every elm is familiarly said to get its man."

Lord Sanderlake winced, and his heart gave an uncomfortable jump. "How many elms are there near the house?" he asked, hoarsely.

"Five, my lord, not including the small wych-elm by the east wing, which can hardly constitute a danger."

"Five, eh? Then see to it that every one of them is felled. Tomorrow."

"Very well, my lord," said Davidson, grinning and drunk with power. "And what are your lordship's wishes regarding the timber?"

"The timber?" mumbled Lord Sanderlake, looking vague.

"It won't be without a certain value," Davidson assured him, "particularly in an agricultural district such as this. As your lordship is no doubt aware, no other wood is suitable for making the hubs of wagon-wheels and, in fact, I believe the rule is elm for the hubs, oak for the spokes and ash for the felloes——"

Lord Sanderlake suddenly lowed like a menaced bull and sank back into his chair. "Davidson——" he began, then broke off with the realisation that no words could adequately express his exasperation. He often asked himself why he kept the fellow, but the question was always a rhetorical one. The truth was that Davidson knew too much to be lightly dismissed. In fact, Lord Sanderlake sometimes suspected that he knew *everything*.

"Yes, my lord?"

"Nothing," said Lord Sanderlake. "Except that a Mr. Digby Cox and his brother will be calling shortly and you can show them up as soon as they arrive. However, don't leave me alone with them until I give you the word. That's all."

As soon as the newspaper-baron was alone, his thoughts returned to his erstwhile science editor. "A message from Pollenport?" he murmured, but what exactly did that portend? Did it mean that Pollenport was back on Earth? Or was he on that hypothetical planet Antigeos? Or was he in space?

Lord Sanderlake's gaze went to the red telephone and for some moments he played with the idea of ringing the office and telling them to stand by for drastic action. He had a predilection for impinging himself upon the workings of his newspaper with dramatic suddenness; and to scream at his harassed chief editor "Kill the front page!" was his idea of good fun, but sober reflection told him that in this case he would hardly be justified. It was still barely six o'clock and even if the news-break did prove as sensational as Digby Cox claimed there would still be plenty of time to re-organise the paper's make-up, and if there was one thing that Lord Sanderlake liked better than screaming "Kill the front page!" at six o'clock, it was screaming "Kill the front page!" at eight o'clock. Besides, for all he knew, the Cox brothers might never turn up. They might be simply pranksters. Or lunatics.

However, the Coxes did turn up, and as Davidson showed them into the room Lord Sanderlake was relieved to notice that neither bore any visible signs of mental derangement. Digby in particular had a serious and sensible face, and there was a sobriety about his bearing and clothes that the newspaper-proprietor found infinitely reassuring. The younger brother, it was true, was untidier and more rugged-looking, but, after a moment's scrutiny, Lord Sanderlake decided that he too was all right, and so dismissed Davidson with a nod.

The suspense was becoming unendurable and it was that that decided him not to offer the Coxes a drink. He felt that there wasn't a moment to waste and, as soon as the three of them were seated, he brought up the matter of Pollenport. "Where the devil is he?" he asked.

"On Antigeos," said Digby.

Lord Sanderlake looked incredulous. "Yet you've had a message from him, you say?"

"Yes. You see, my brother and I own a small electrical engineering business at Brydd," he said, "but our real interests lie somewhat further afield. To be perfectly frank, we've practically bankrupted ourselves in astronomical research."

"What, telescopes and so on?"

"Not exactly, but, Lord Sanderlake, do you know anything of blind astronomy?"

"What, radaroscopy? Well, I know the principle of it; and that's what you've been indulging yourselves in, is it?"

"Yes, and just lately we've been doing some special research on sun-spot activity, using a particularly sensitive receiver. And this afternoon my brother found himself picking up morse on a wave-length where no morse could be."

Lord Sanderlake glanced from Digby to Bryan, and back again. "From Pollenport?" he whispered.

"Yes," said Digby and, as he spoke, he drew an envelope from his pocket. It it was a short length of recording tape together with the text of Pollenport's message.

"Have you a tape-recorder here?" he asked.

"Yes," said Lord Sanderlake, with a glance towards his desk. "That's a recording of the message, is it?"

"It is. Of course, it doesn't prove anything, because we could easily have faked it, but we thought you might like to hear it."

"Certainly I should," said Lord Sanderlake, and took the tape. He went across to his desk and opened a deep drawer in which was a tape-recorder.

Davidson came in, ostensibly to make up the fire, just as the stutter of Pollenport's morse started to emerge from the drawer and Lord Sanderlake stopped the machine. "Know anything about morse, Davidson?" he asked.

The butler bowed assent. "I must admit to a certain familiarity with it, my lord," he murmured. "When I was hall-boy in His Grace's service I was enrolled as a scout in the troop attached to the estate. In fact, I rose to be the patrol-leader of the Buffaloes, and among my proficiency-badges I numbered one for morse."

"H'mph. Well, see what you can make of this."

He switched on the machine again and Davidson listened attentively. As the import of the message dawned on him, he glanced at the Coxes and smiled superciliously.

"Well?" muttered Lord Sanderlake, as the tape came to an end.

"It's a message from Professor Pollenport on the planet Antigeos, my lord," said Davidson. "Or, at least, that's what it purports to be. It merely requests anyone receiving the message to acknowledge it on the same wave-length." He gazed into space for a moment, then added unexpectedly, "Yes, of course—it was your lordship who instigated the Pollenport Expedition, wasn't it?"

"That's right, Davidson. But for me there wouldn't have been any expedition."

Davidson returned to the fire, but went on talking. "I've always considered it a pity that the enterprise was taken over by commercial interests in its later stages," he murmured. "In fact, they even sent a representative to accompany the expedition, did they not? A military gentleman. A Major —— no, I'm afraid the name escapes me for the moment."

Lord Sanderlake glanced up from the text of Pollenport's message. "That's enough, Davidson. Do whatever you have to do, and leave us."

Davidson swept the hearth meticulously, then retreated. However, it was seldom that he did not permit himself the last word, and now, as he closed the door, he murmured: "Ah, the name's returned to me now, my lord. It was, of course, Major Stewart McQuoid!"

Lord Sanderlake frowned irritably, and handed the message back to Digby. "Could it be a hoax?" he asked.

"Unlikely," said Digby, and gave his reasons.

"Yet you made no attempt to reply?"

"We couldn't," Digby told him. "We've no transmitter nearly powerful enough, nor any means of building one. As I've already mentioned, we're broke and our credit is exhausted."

Lord Sanderlake jumped up and started pacing the room. Outside, the wind howled and blustered, but now all his fears were forgotten. He saw himself as having the century's greatest news-story within his grasp and his sole thought was how best to handle it.

"You've told no one else?" he asked.

"No one."

"Then what are the chances of this message being picked up by some other chap?"

"Small," said Digby. "In fact, I should say that they're about a million to one against."

"Good." Lord Sanderlake returned to his chair. "Now I'll tell you what we'll do. We three are the only people in the world who know about this, so we'll just keep our mouths shut and go to work. How much do you owe?"

"Between three and four hundred."

"Then have the bills sent to me, and order all the equipment you want. And how long will it take you to build this transmitter?"

Digby and Bryan exchanged glances. "A fortnight," said Bryan. "If we work at it day and night."

Digby smiled. "I think that's a little optimistic," he murmured, "but shall we say three weeks?"

"Right!" said Lord Sanderlake. "And now we come to the question of your remuneration and I'll tell you what I'll do. If you succeed in communicating with Pollenport within three weeks I'll pay you—" he hesitated, biting his thumb-nail—"I'll pay you two thousand pounds! How's that?"

"Excellent," said Digby, and they shook on it.

Then Lord Sanderlake touched the bell, and when Davidson opened the door, everything seemed to happen at once. A window burst open and a gale of wind came streaming in, lifting the curtain and filling the room with its force. For a moment Lord Sanderlake stood as if transfixed, then his mouth dropped open and he slid to the floor with a crash.

"Ah, swooned," remarked Davidson, and went to him. He loosened Lord Sanderlake's collar and somewhat roughly pushed his head down between his knees.

"Shall I pour out some whisky?" asked Digby.

"Hardly necessary, I think, sir," said Davidson. "He's hyperthyroid, you know, and certain things upset him. Cats, for instance, and—" he glanced towards the window which Bryan was struggling to close—"and storms. Nervous, in fact, like all these new creations."

Chapter II

I

THE view from the hillside window was dazzling in its splendour. Timothy Penn, sitting in the silent room for a tenth part of each Antigean day, never tired of its beauty. The Earth could offer nothing comparable, and the Antigean word for that part of the northern continent could be translated roughly as 'the Land of Fountains' or 'the Land of Many Waters'.

It was on the sea-coast to the east of the great desert and for centuries it had been preserved as a beauty spot on account of its hundreds of geysers and natural fountains. From his window Timothy had a perfect view of the whole valley, which was divided into two by a river as broad as the Thames at Tilbury. The grass of the valley was greener than any he remembered ever seeing on the Earth, just as the waters of the river were clearer, but for all that he was homesick, almost despairingly so. He gazed past the sparkling forest of fountains towards the sun and, squinting at it, dreamt of his native planet, much as five years before he had dreamt of Antigeos while idling in Hyde Park and blinking into the sun's glare.

He grinned a little ruefully at the recollection, but told himself stoutly that even if he had known all that was in store for him, he would still have come—yes, even if the worst came to the worst and he had to spend the rest of his life in an alien world. It had been an enchanted adventure and, in any case, if he had not embarked upon it, he would never have met and married Rose Pollenport. He felt that almost any fate would be bearable as long as he had Rose.

The amplifier at his side muttered and crackled, and he glanced at it, but the hope that had burned so fiercely when six weeks before they had first started to transmit signals to the Earth was now almost too dead to be revived. Either the signals were not getting through or they were not being picked up, and not only Timothy but the others as well were beginning to think the experiment a failure. For every minute of the day the signals were going out, but day after day the receiving amplifier stayed silent except for atmospherics and the crackle of static.

Just then Rose came in with Prue, their small daughter. "We're a little early——" she began, then broke off when she saw that Timothy had his ear to the amplifier.

He smiled at her and shook his head. "It's nothing," he told her, getting up. "Just the usual buzz and crackle. It begins to look as if we've had all the trouble of learning morse for nothing, doesn't it?"

"Oh, it'll probably come in useful some time," murmured Rose, slipping into the chair that Timothy had vacated. "When we get back to the Earth you'll be able to start a troop of Boy Scouts or something."

"When we get back to the Earth!" muttered Timothy bleakly. "That's a laugh."

Prue, who was a solid and forthright child, announced that she wanted to see her grandpa. "I've got a shell for him," she said, and Rose explained that they'd been on the beach.

"So you have," said Timothy, dutifully examining the shell. "But it's still got the winkle in it."

"Yes," agreed Prue. "I've got a shell and a winkle for him. We going to see him?"

"All right. That is, if we can find him."

"He said something about going over to the site," observed Rose. "Actually, he's on duty next, so if you like to go over there, taking your time, you can pick him up and come back with him." Then, in a different voice, she added: "Oh, Tim, I wish you hadn't said that!"

"Said what?" asked Timothy, surprised.

"Well, you implied that we'd never get back to the Earth, didn't you? And it's depressed me."

Timothy put an arm round her and stroked her hair. "Oh, we'll get back all right," he assured her. "Of course we shall."

"Yes, but we've been saying that for the last three years. Ever since Daddy, Sam and Paul got back from the other continent."

"I know, but, after all, a spaceship is being built."

"Yes, and they've been building it for the last two years," muttered Rose bitterly. "They're so slow, darling, but, of course, it's all right for them. They've got longer life-spans than we have. And anyway they live here!"

Timothy patted her shoulder, but she swung her chair round impatiently, so that his hand dropped to his side. "Sweetheart, you don't seem to realise what's happening," she cried. "When we came to Antigeos, I was a girl, and now I'm a woman! And when we leave, if ever, I'll be a crone!"

"What's a crone?" asked Prue.

"What your Mummy sees when she looks in the glass," Rose told her, and Timothy kissed the top of his wife's head and remarked that she was talking nonsense.

"What's a crone?" Prue persisted.

"An old, old, old lady——" began Rose, then broke off suddenly as the amplifier started crackling on a different note.

"Morse?" she whispered, and for a few moments the two adults were held spellbound.

"What's morse?" asked Prue, and her parents hushed her with a vehemence such as she had never encountered in all her four years' existence. Startled, she glanced from one to the other and Timothy hurriedly took her hand to check the threat of tears, and at the same moment the crackling resolved itself into meaningless atmospherics.

"False alarm," he murmured, and moved towards the door. "Come on, Prue. Let's go and find Grandpa."

"Grandpa!" shouted Prue gaily and, reassured, she broke away from Timothy and led the way along the brilliantly-lit subterranean corridor. All the humans had been living in this particular habitation for the last two years and, as far as Prue was concerned, it was the only home she could remember. In fact, she was even more familiar with the habitation's labyrinth of corridors, roller-esplanades and public rooms than were her parents, and every Antigeosian living in the place was her friend. Most of the Antigeosians spoke some English and so far it had not, of course, occurred to Prue that they were different in kind from the humans.

On their way out of the habitation they had to pass through one of the bathing-halls and as soon as Prue recognised some of her friends in the pools she wavered in her purpose. "May I swim, Daddy?" she asked. "There's Puck and Mab!"

"Yes, you can swim if you like," said Timothy. "We've got plenty of time."

With a single movement she pulled off her tunic and went prancing towards the nearest pool.

"No, not in there!" cried Timothy. "You know Mummy doesn't like you to go in that one."

Prue turned, scowling. "Why doesn't she?"

"Because it's too hot for you."

"Then why's Puck in it?"

Timothy hesitated, considering how to explain to a four-year-old that Antigeosians have higher body-temperatures than ours and can stand hotter water.

"Is it because he's a boy?" asked Prue.

"Yes, I expect that's it," said Timothy, desperately. "Anyway, be a good girl and go in the other pool."

"But Mab's not a boy," Prue informed him, and at that moment, to Timothy's relief, the two little Anti-geosans caught sight of Prue and, clambering out of the pool, joined her. All three were about of a size and it amused Timothy to watch them as they gravely con-ferred. It was difficult to say just how they communi-cated. Neither Puck nor Mab had more than a few chance words of English, yet, as far as Prue was con-cerned, they seemed to be able to make themselves understood all right and Timothy sometimes wondered if perhaps his daughter had acquired some knowledge of the Antigean gesture language. It was an absurd idea, of course, since no one could understand the gesture language who lacked the frontal antennæ that were a characteristic of the Antigeosians, but in Timothy's eyes Prue was an exceptional child and one not to be judged by mundane standards.

The conference ended with the three babies advanc-ing hand-in-hand towards one of the cooler pools—Prue's pink body flanked by two golden ones—and as they splashed down the steps into the water Timothy turned away and sat himself at one of the tables by the wall. He helped himself to a mango-like fruit, and a grey-clad waitress came to him and asked him if there was anything else he wanted.

He did not recognise the girl and was surprised by how good her English was. Many of the waitresses, coming from distant habitations for their work-periods, spoke no English and, when Timothy had ordered wine, he asked her where she had learned it.

"I make study," she assured him, with a broad smile. "I study English almost from the first day you came. I live in the Land of Lions, where your spaceship came down."

Timothy smiled but he was saddened by the thought of how long ago it all seemed. He could no longer disguise the fact that Rose and he were tired and oppressed by the length of time their exile had lasted. The strain of living among a people more alien to them than any people on Earth was beginning to tell on them, and the thought that they might have to endure it until the end of their lives was a nightmare.

The other three—Jonah Pollenport, Sam Spencross and Paul Greenwood—were not affected by homesickness to the same extent, and indeed their whole attitude was different. They had formed the crew of the spaceship, men doing a job and professionally prepared for all the hazards of that job, whereas Timothy and Rose had both been caught up into this enforced exile by their own foolhardiness. Timothy had bought his passage on the spaceship with the winnings of a football pool, and Rose had come as a stowaway, and no misfortunes are harder to bear than those we bring upon ourselves as the result of our folly.

He sipped his wine and watched Prue swimming round the pool with all the vigour of a tadpole. "Rose and I must have been mad!" he told himself, burdened by his sense of responsibility for Prue. That Rose and he might be condemned to a lifetime of exile was one thing, but that they should have brought a child into that alien world to share their exile was surely in the nature of an enormity. Or so it seemed to Timothy in his prevailing mood.

"God, what will become of her?" he wondered, and then closed his mind to the subject as he had closed it often before. . . .

It had been Pollenport's idea to try and establish radio-communication with the Earth and perhaps he had suggested it when he saw that homesickness was daily getting a stronger hold upon his daughter and son-in-law. The Antigeosians had, of course, supplied all the materials, but both the transmission-unit and the receiving set had been built solely by the humans, and for weeks their excitement had been intense. All five of them had learnt the morse code, practising it assiduously and tapping out messages for each other at every opportunity, and then had come the day when the transmitter was ready. They had all of them been rather naïve about it, expecting to get a reply right away, and when days passed and no reply came, their disappointment had been correspondingly great.

"It's just not getting through!" he told himself, as he finished his wine. "If it were getting through, someone somewhere would have picked it up," and he wondered if presently the Antigeosians would agree to their building an even more powerful transmitter. . . .

II

Prue flung her inconsiderable weight against the controlling lever, and the rail-car rolled forward. "I began

26

it!" she screamed, almost beside herself with excitement. "You didn't help, did you?"

"No," Timothy assured her. "But you didn't begin it—you started it."

"Yes, I started it! Didn't I?"

Sunlight fell across their faces as the car came out into the open, and the pointsman in his little kiosk glanced at Timothy inquiringly. Timothy pointed across the valley and the man nodded and threw a switch. The car rattled over the points, then, gathering speed, ran down into the valley and started threading its way between the fountains and geysers.

"That's Silver Maiden!" cried Prue, pointing to one of the most beautiful fountains of all—a single slender column of water that shot nearly a hundred feet up into the air before it shattered into a plume that flashed and sparkled in the sunlight.

Prue, lolling back on the car's cushioned seat, gazed at the wonderful fountain and sighed with satisfaction. "Mab told me a story about Silver Maiden," she said.

"Oh? And what was it?"

"I don't know," said Prue, losing interest. She tried to look at the sun and sneezed.

"I sneezed," she told Timothy.

"So I heard. You tried to look at the sun, and that's why you sneezed."

"Is it nice there?" she asked.

"Where?"

"There," she said vaguely, and gestured towards the sun.

"I don't know what you mean, darling."

"Well, where Mummy says," she told him, and then Timothy began to understand.

"Did Mummy tell you we were going somewhere?" he asked.

"Yes. When we were on the beach, she told me."

"Ah, I see. She told you we might be going to a place on the other side of the sun, did she?"

Prue looked uncertain, but nodded. "Is it nice there?" she asked again.

"Well, it's different," said Timothy, thinking nostalgically of fog and rain and the grey sky over London. "But I expect you'll like it. There'll be lots of other little girls and boys there who you can talk to and play with."

"Will Puck and Mab be there?"

Timothy had to admit that that was improbable, and Prue's face took on an obstinate look. "Then I don't want to go," she said, and her tone indicated that the matter was closed.

The rail-car rumbled across the bridge that spanned the river, and the vapour from a geyser on the farther bank drifted damply across their faces. Prue informed Timothy that the geyser's name was Old Goat, then embarked on a story concerning the geyser and Silver Maiden.

"He wanted to marry her, you see," she said, "but Silver Maiden's daddy didn't like Old Goat, so he turned him into a geyser and put him on one side of the river and he turned Silver Maiden into a fountain and put her on the other side of the river. Then Old Goat couldn't marry Silver Maiden, so that was all right."

"That's the story Mab told you, is it?"

"Yes."

"But how did she tell you?"

"She told me," said Prue, and left Timothy mystified as before. In fact, he decided after some reflection, the only possible explanation was that Prue could understand something of the gesture language *visually,*

28

a feat that was totally beyond any of the adult humans.

Now the rail-car was approaching the long line of low hills that bounded the valley and Prue asked if they would be going through the tunnel.

"Yes," said Timothy and, moving closer to him, she took a firm grip of his thumb.

"You don't like the tunnel, do you?" he murmured.

"Yes, I do like it," she assured him, bravely. "And it's only a pretence tunnel, isn't it?"

"What do you mean?"

"Well, it can't hurt me, can it?"

"No, of course it can't hurt. Why, you've been through it dozens of times with me, and with Mummy, and with Grandpa, haven't you, and it's never hurt you yet?"

"No. It's only a pretence tunnel."

As she spoke, the rail-car trundled down a short cutting and plunged into the tunnel's darkness. Her grip on Timothy's thumb tightened and he rather suspected that she had her eyes closed. Actually, she knew less of darkness than if she had been born and brought up on the Earth—the habitations were always lighted and she had never been out at night—and her fear of it was inexplicable. It worried Timothy and he sometimes wondered how, if they ever succeeded in returning to the Earth, Prue would adjust herself to its rigours.

"Still, that's a bridge we can cross when we come to it," he told himself. "And at the rate things are going, we may never come to it."

He was thinking of the spaceship that the Antigeosians were building and which he and Prue were on their way to visit. Frankly, he had his doubts about the whole project and, what was more significant, so had Sam Spencross. Yet all that Sam, or any of the humans, really knew about it was that it was different from

c

any spaceship that had ever been conceived on the Earth.

That a spaceship should be under construction at all represented a revolution in Antigean principles, and its inception dated back to the time when the Antigeosians had re-built the *Skylark* for Pollenport and his companions. That experiment had failed, but it had influenced the higher councils into thinking along the lines of space travel, with the result that, two years before they had produced plans for a spaceship of their own. They had heard enough about the Earth from Pollenport to see it as a source of potential danger to the Antigean way of life, and now their idea was to send an expedition to investigate at first hand. About twenty Antigeosians, all English-speaking, were going to make the voyage, but so far the humans had not been able to obtain an approximate date of departure. When they questioned the engineers on the point the only answer they got was, "Soon", and that, by Antigean standards, might mean anything up to thirty years.

Prue's grip on Timothy's thumb relaxed and then he realised that the darkest part of the tunnel was behind them; and within a few moments the rail-car shot out into the sunlight. The valley they were now entering could hardly have been more different from the one they had just left, and Timothy shaded his eyes against the glare beating down from the parched rocks and buttes. The place was almost a desert, and the sand with which its floor was covered was the colour of curry-powder.

The heat was appalling and for about the hundredth time Timothy asked himself why the Antigeosians had chosen to build their spaceship in such a forbidding spot. He could see the construction site about half a mile ahead of him. It was surmounted by the vast bulging disc that was to form the spaceship's hull, and in the shadow of the disc a few dozen Antigeosians were working at various tasks.

Prue clambered up on the rail-car's seat and grasped the controlling-lever. "Stop?" she asked, but Timothy shook his head.

"Not quite yet. We don't want to walk any farther than we need in this heat."

The hull of the projected spaceship was immense— easily a thousand feet in diameter—and so thick vertically that from Timothy's angle it looked more nearly a sphere than a disc. Like Saturn, it was encircled by two huge rings on the plane of its horizontal circumference, but what their purpose was the humans could only guess at. The Antigeosians either would not or could not explain and, although they had courteously shown their guests over the construction, the tour of inspection had left the humans little the wiser, for so far the spaceship was no more than an empty shell honeycombed by compartments. The great disc, supported at four points by stunted towers of scaffolding, remained an enigma to them, and merely evidence, in the very scale of its conception, to the immense stores of technical knowledge locked away in the Antigean archives.

"Now?" asked Prue and, when Timothy nodded, dragged the lever back with all her strength.

The rail-car came to a jerky standstill and Timothy swung himself over the side. He lifted his daughter down, then leant back into the car and threw the lever forward again. Unattended, the rail-car trundled merrily away from them to be dealt with by the first pointsman it came to.

It was cooler in the shadow of the spaceship and, as Timothy and Prue strolled across to the site, they came upon Sam Spencross seated on the sand with Quince,

31

Horatio and another Antigeosian. He did not look up as they approached, because he was giving all his attention to something that Horatio was explaining to him and his gaze was resting on an elaborate diagram that the Antigeosian was drawing in the sand.

Sam's Antigean sojourn had changed him remarkably little. He was a cautious, solid man and it was simply not in his nature to change much, whatever the circumstances. Always a conservative in matters of dress, he still wore the trousers and leather shoes that he had arrived in—the trousers as shiny as the shoes, and considerably patched—and, although he now wore an Antigean tunic in place of a shirt, it was a decorously white one, and the tie he wore with it betokened membership of the South Norwood Cricket Club.

Prue's patience was short-lived. "Where's Grandpa?" she asked, and Sam glanced up.

"Why, hullo, you two," he said. "How's tricks?"

"Nothing to report. And what are you doing—playing noughts-and-crosses?"

Sam chuckled. "Looks like it, doesn't it? But the fact is that old Horatio here has been coming out of his shell a bit. He's been telling me a few things about the spaceship, and it wouldn't be puting it too high to say I'm intrigued."

"You mean, you think it may even take off one day?"

"Oh, I wouldn't go so far as to say that," murmured Sam, grinning, "but, for all that, they've got hold of some interesting theories."

"Where's Grandpa?" asked Prue again, and this time she was not to be denied. No one knew quite where Pollenport was, but presently Timothy found him playing chess against Paul Greenwood in the shadow of a large rock.

32

Prue presented her grandfather with the winkle-shell. "There's a winkle in it," she told him, "and his name's Prue, like mine."

Pollenport thanked her and kissed her. "I've always wanted a shell-fish called Prue," he assured her, then glanced at Timothy. "You're early, aren't you? I thought I had an hour or more in hand."

"Oh, we haven't come to fetch you. We just looked along to see what was happening."

"Nothing's happening except that Paul is beating me," said Pollenport, and Timothy took Prue on his lap and settled down to watch the game.

The years on Antigeos had left their mark on Pollenport. His shock of hair was almost white now, and his face was more lined. He still lived in the faith that one day they would all return to the Earth, but Timothy often wondered if perhaps that faith were not wearing rather thin and noticed that Pollenport no longer collected scientific data with anything like his former zest. He had had the main responsibility all along and nowadays there were times when he looked a weary and defeated man.

Paul Greenwood, except that he had put on weight, was much what he had always been—a tall, loose-limbed, easy-going Negro, with the faith of a Mark Tapley in cheerfulness as an antidote to adversity. In fact, he frequently remarked that Antigean life suited him to a T. "Nothing to do except lie in the sun all day, eating when we're hungry and sleeping when we're tired," he said. "Why, I guess we'd be crazy to go back to the Earth again, even if we had the chance!" But when he talked like that Timothy surmised that his words betokened an attempt to make the best of a bad job more than they expressed what he really felt.

Paul moved a pawn and discovered check on Pollenport's king. "I think that about does it," he murmured. "Mate in four, I guess."

"Nonsense," snorted Pollenport. "My knight can——"

However, what his knight could do was never disclosed, for neither the sentence nor the game were ever to be finished. For at that moment he heard Sam Spencross calling his name with breathless urgency and jumped up to see Sam pounding across the site accompanied by a young Antigean girl.

"Jonah!" yelled Sam. "It's happened! A signal from the Earth. . . ." and then Pollenport noticed that the girl had a scrap of paper in her hand.

It was a message from Rose, and, with Paul and Timothy looking over his shoulder, he read: "Daddy, I've just picked up the following signal—'This is Digby Cox on the planet Earth calling Jonah Pollenport on the planet Antigeos. Your signal has been received by amateurs at Brydd, England, and we await your further communication.' This message is still repeating itself, and now what price miracles? Rose."

For a couple of seconds there was silence, then Pollenport gave an uncertain laugh. "England," he muttered. "My God, how wonderful!"

CHAPTER III

I

DESPITE his double-barrelled name, Gordon Keble-Keith was a modest man and he did not believe in drawing unnecessary attention to either himself or his activities. His offices in Leadenhall Street were limited to three rooms rather shabbily furnished, and few people knew much of what went on behind their dingy walls.

Keble-Keith had the reputation of being an enormously wealthy man, but no one would have suspected it from his appearance. All the available evidence suggested that he only had one suit, one overcoat and one hat, and his brief-case was so worn, shapeless and nondescript that he never stood in any danger of having it snatched from him by a bandit. Yet there had been times when he could not have exchanged that brief-case for a king's ransom, and shown a profit.

Those times were in the past, however, and now, though no one knew it but himself, Keble-Keith was in low water. Five years before, he had over-reached himself, and since that time confidence in his advice and his example had steadily declined. The Midas touch had deserted him and now daily he was preoccupied by visions of total downfall and disaster. He thought of himself in heroic terms and frequently reflected that soon there would be nothing for it but to fall on his sword—his sword, in that event, being represented by an overdose of sleeping tablets.

Actually, he had not the look of a hero. He was a sandy man, and rather unkempt. His hair overlapped his collar at the back in limp scallops, and his moustache, which was a shade lighter than his hair, looked as if he were given to chewing it. His eyes, behind their sandy lashes, were a watery blue, and the pallor of his long face was only relieved by a dyspeptic redness round the tip of his nose.

He was an assiduous reader of *The Times,* especially of its front page, and his first task on arriving at the office each morning was to make a detailed study of the Personal Column. In fact, he had picked up many stimulating items of information from it in the course of his career, and the most startling advertisement of all was the one that met his eye on a damp, foggy morning in December, 1973. He read the advertisement twice, then broke out into such a noticeable sweat that he had to wipe his brow with his handkerchief. Then he took up a pencil, drew a heavy line round the insertion and rang for his secretatry.

She was in the room almost before his finger had left the bell-push and he passed her the newspaper. "Miss Spooner, take a letter to this advertiser," he said, "and have it sent round to *The Times* by hand right away. 'Dear Sir, My attention has been drawn to your advertisement in today's *Times,* and I should be glad if you would communicate with me at your earliest convenience. Yours faithfully. . . .' That's all."

Miss Spooner made a note of the box-number and returned the newspaper to her employer. As she left him, he took another glance at the advertisement and his desiccated heart swelled a little within him.

He read:

Major Stewart McQuoid. Advertiser can give information as to whereabouts of this gentleman to bona-fide inquirers.

Keble-Keith's gaze travelled from the paper to the fog-choked window. "Five years!" he mused, and all but laughed with excitement. Five years had passed since Stewart McQuoid set off in that crazy spaceship, and now came—this.

Antigeos had meant different things to different people and to Keble-Keith it had meant the New Imperialism. Some day someone was going to make himself immortal by annexing a planet, and Keble-Keith had dreamed that that someone might be he. . . .

II

The next twenty-four hours proved the most trying of Keble-Keith's life, but at about half-past twelve the following morning Miss Spooner came to him to tell him that the advertiser was in her office. "He won't give his name," she said, "but he's got your letter all right. Shall I show him in?"

"Yes," said Keble-Keith, almost soundlessly. He had a lump in his throat the size of a hen's egg and it was as much as he could do to talk at all.

His visitor turned out to be a big man in his late forties, with large features and a saturnine expression. He was dark and ponderous, and in some fashion managed to be both obsequious and imposing at the same time. The buttons of his double-breasted overcoat struck Keble-Keith as being too large, his gloves too yellow, and the brim of his bowler hat too curly, and, after a moment's hesitation, Keble-Keith decided to ignore the man's proffered hand.

"Sit down, Mr.—er——" he said. "I don't believe I know your name, do I?"

"I think not," agreed the big man, sitting down, "and, for the time being, I would prefer to preserve my anonymity. In any case, my name is irrelevant."

Keble-Keith shrugged and offered his visitor a cigarette, which was accepted. Then he struck a match and said, with a casualness he was far from feeling, "So you have news of Major McQuoid, have you?"

"Possibly, but first there is the question of your bona fides. May I ask what occasions your interest in that gentleman?"

Keble-Keith swallowed hard and stiffened. "I'm interested in Major McQuoid," he said, "because he happens to be an employee of mine—or, at least, of a company of which I am managing director."

"And may I inquire the name of the company?"

"The Anglo-Antigean Development Corporation," said Keble-Keith, with a certain terseness. "You may not know it, but it was that company which financed the Pollenport Expedition."

"Oh? And not the *Daily Messenger*?"

"Certainly not the *Daily Messenger*," snapped Keble-Keith. "Admittedly, Lord Sanderlake instigated the expedition, but when it came to financing it, he was practically a non-starter. When he backed out, my associates and I stepped into the breach and put up the necessary funds on the condition that we were represented on the expedition by Major McQuoid." He paused, and straightened his blotter. "Well, I think you'll agree that those circumstances give me a valid interest in McQuoid's fate, but if you want documentary evidence——"

The sentence trailed off into silence and for some moments the two men gazed at each other across the desk. Then the big man cleared his throat and said that he was prepared to accept Keble-Keith's word.

"And that brings us to the question of terms," he observed. "What's your idea?"

Keble-Keith smiled and remarked that that depended entirely upon the nature of the information.

"Naturally," said the big man, "but I'm running a risk in coming here at all, if you understand me, and that risk demands its equivalent. In fact, I won't open my mouth again for less than five thousand."

Keble-Keith pulled open a drawer of his desk and took out a cheque-book. He scribbled a cheque for five thousand pounds, signed it and pushed it across to his visitor. "You can fill in your name yourself," he said. "Now give me your information and, if I'm satisfied with it, the cheque's yours. And, having reached this stage, I really don't see why you shouldn't give me your name."

"It's Davidson," said the big man, with his eyes on the cheque. "Robert Davidson."

The cheque fascinated him. He had never seen such a big one before, and he was overawed. He had come prepared to haggle, with five hundred as his minimum, but now he was wishing he had asked ten thousand.

"Well, Mr. Davidson," said Keble-Keith, "where is Major McQuoid?"

Davidson wrenched his gaze from the cheque, and grinned. "He's on the planet Antigeos," he said.

Keble-Keith drew breath sharply and a dreamy look came into his eyes. "Then it *does* exist?" he whispered.

"Certainly it exists," said Davidson. "You see, it so happens that I'm employed as major-domo by an influential nobleman, and some five or six weeks ago two young radar experts arrived to see him on important business. I was not present at the early part of the interview, but later I was called in to decode a certain message in morse. As a matter of fact, it was on a tape-recording and I understood that the young men had picked it up from the ether by means of an ultra-short-wave receiving set. I listened to it, and I doubt if any-one can imagine my astonishment when I realised I was hearing a message from Professor Pollenport on the planet Antigeos."

"Could have been faked," muttered Keble-Keith.

"It could have been, but it wasn't," Davidson assured him. "Since that time, regular communication has been established and the two young men are supplying my employer with almost daily bulletins of news from Antigeos."

"And McQuoid's with Pollenport, is he?"

"On that point I'm afraid I have no certain informa-tion," said Davidson. "At the risk of appearing dis-loyal, I must admit that my employer has a suspicious nature and does not take me fully into his confidence, with the result that my sources of information are limited to telephone conversations accidentally over-heard and such-like contingencies. I have, however, gathered that Antigeos is enormously rich in natural resources and that it is inhabited by a mild and amenable people."

Metaphorically, Keble-Keith's mouth watered and he coughed briefly to hide his excitement. "Now I think you'd better tell me who your employer is," he said. "I probably know him."

Davidson's face darkened and an obstinate look came into his eyes. "I'll give you that information when the cheque has been cashed," he said. "Or don't you trust me?"

40

"But of course," he murmured, and drew the cheque towards him. He opened it, wrote in Davidson's name, then returned it to him.

"My bank's only five minutes away," he said, "and as soon as you've got the money you can ring me and give me your employer's name."

Both men rose and Keble-Keith followed Davidson across the room. "So I'll be hearing from you in about fifteen minutes?" he murmured, as he opened the door.

"Certainly," said Davidson, and it did not seem to occur to him that Keble-Keith was being quite extraordinarily trusting.

Keble-Keith waited until he heard the outer door close, then rang for his secretary.

She appeared and he told her to telephone the bank immediately. "Instruct them to stop payment on Cheque No. 164614," he said, "and, when you've done that, send young Ashwell in to me and go and have your lunch."

Keble-Keith was feeling happier than he'd felt for months and when, a few minutes later, Mr. Cyril Ashwell came into his room, his spirits rose still further.

"Ah, Ashwell," he said, with a faint smile, "I was just asking myself whether you'd care to earn a small bonus by means of your incidental talents. In fact, five pounds was the sum I had in mind."

"I should be most gr-gr-grateful, s-s-sir," stammered Ashwell. "Wh-wh-what is it you w-w-wish?"

He was a weedy young man and, as far as his appearance was concerned, there was little to distinguish him from several thousand other City clerks. Yet, as Keble-Keith had suggested, he was a man of unusual parts and this was not the first time he had been employed in a special capacity.

"Miss Spooner is just going to lunch," said Keble-Keith, "and I want you to take her place on the reception desk. Within the next fifteen minutes, a large, swarthy man called Davidson will probably show up and it's my guess that he will be a little cross. He will ask to see me and you will tell him that I've been called away to Paris unexpectedly and won't be back for a month. At that point he will probably try to force his way into this office and you will—er—er. . . . Well, you will, won't you, Ashwell?"

"Of c-course, sir. And it w-w-will be a pl-pleasure."

"Good. And now could you ask Miss Willis to come in for a moment?"

If Ashwell was indistinguishable from several thousand City clerks, Miss Willis was indistinguishable from several tens of thousand City typists, middle-aged ones. She was the epitome of insignificance and, even when she was standing in front of Keble-Keith's desk, he could hardly realise she was there.

He told her that he had a small job for her. "Yes, Miss Willis—one similar to the one you did in connection with my wife. My former wife, I should say."

"Oh, yes, sir?"

"In a few minutes' time I'm expecting a Mr. Davidson to call on me, but I shan't see him. He will come and he will go, and when he leaves the premises I want you to follow him. Don't lose sight of him for a moment and, in particular, find out where he lives and who employs him. When you've tracked him to his lair, and not until then, ring me and give me the news. Can you do that, do you think?"

"Yes, I think so, sir, and anyway you can rest assured that I'll do my utmost."

Keble-Keith took out his wallet and handed her two

five-pound notes. "These are for your expenses," he said, "and any change there is you can keep. In any case, you're to have five pounds clear."

Miss Willis thanked him and was gone like a ghost. Keble-Keith locked the door behind her and returned dreamily to his desk. He sat and doodled, listening for sounds of strife from the outer office. *"Antigeos! . . . Antigeos! . . . Antigeos! . . ."* sang his pulses and then he suddenly came to himself to discover that he had written, "Gordon Keble-Keith, 1st Baron Antigeos," no fewer than seven times on his blotter.

He blushed a little and was carefully scoring out the words when he heard the outer door burst open. He stiffened, sitting upright in his chair. No one, he reflected, would ever have suspected young Ashwell of being an expert in judo, a black-belt in fact, but, in view of his puniness and his stammer, it was, of course, understandable.

The deep rumble of Davidson's voice came to his ears, followed, almost inaudibly, by Ashwell's gentle and con- ciliatory tones.

"Paris!" roared Davidson, in a voice that might have been heard for a mile. "Paris, you say? H'm, we'll see about that!"

Keble-Keith heard him stride across the outer office. The door-handle rattled briefly, then Ashwell must have gone into action. There came a crash as of a cosmic collision and for a moment Keble-Keith could have sworn that the building shook.

"W-w-want any more?" asked Ashwell shrilly, and the only reply was an uncertain grating noise as Davidson got to his feet.

The short silence that followed was broken by Davidson shakily muttering something about "nothing but a common swindler!"

43

"Th-that'll be enough of th-that," screamed Ashwell, "or next time I'll h-hurt you!"

The outer door slammed, and Keble-Keith took another five pounds out of his wallet. He went into the outer office and found Ashwell standing by the desk gently rubbing his left wrist with a smirk of satisfaction on his face.

"Well done, Ashwell," said Keble-Keith, handing him the five pounds, "but perhaps you'd better hang on for a little, in case he comes back."

"V-v-very good, sir. But I don't think h-h-he'll come back—ev-ev-ever! You see, I threw h-h-him with an *okuriashi h-h-harai,* which can be unpleasant."

"Sounds horrible," agreed Keble-Keith, and went back into his office.

So far operations were going well and his next step was to telephone the brightest of his brokers, a man called Stanley Dutton.

"Stan, do you remember the Anglo-Antigean flotation?" he asked.

Stan groaned. "Shall I ever forget it?" he muttered. "But why bring that up?"

"What do the shares stand at now?"

"They haven't been quoted for years," said Stan, with a hollow laugh, "and my guess is that a five-shilling postal order would buy up the lot."

Keble-Keith lowered his voice. "Well, listen, Stan— I'm moving in on them. I want you to work fast and get me an option on every available share."

"Why, what's up?" asked Stan, with another laugh. "You're not going to tell me that that little dream has come true? Antigeos, I mean."

"Are you crazy? I'm in touch with an interested party, that's all."

"Oh, a mug?" said Stan, with deep understanding.

"Okay, I'll get cracking right away, and I'll have those options before anyone even realises there's a call."

Keble-Keith hung up and when Miss Spooner returned from lunch he was deeply engaged in calculations that were as exciting as they were complex. "Bring me the Anglo-Antigean file," he told her, "and then I don't want to be disturbed for the rest of the afternoon. I'm out to everyone except Miss Willis. When she rings, have her put through right away."

It was getting on for five o'clock before at last Miss Willis came through and by then the cigarette-smoke in the office was nearly as thick as the fog outside.

"I'm sorry I've been so long," she twittered, "but I had to follow our quarry down to the country and he didn't leave London until the public-houses closed. In fact, I think he made himself quite tipsy."

"Where are you now, then?"

"At Bredinge, in Kent," she told him, "and it seems that Mr. Davidson is employed at a big house here called Narraway Towers."

"But that's Lord Sanderlake's place!" exclaimed Keble-Keith, on a rising note.

"Yes, that's right. Mr. Davidson is Lord Sanderlake's butler."

Keble-Keith grinned like a gratified shark. "Well, that's extremely cosy news," he murmured. "And you realise that you're not to breathe a word of this to anyone, don't you?"

"Yes, Mr. Keble-Keith."

III

Lord Sanderlake's office, on the roof of the *Daily Messenger* building, was constructed almost entirely of glass and the effect on a foggy day was eerie. It formed a cave in the fog and now, in the brilliantly-lighted cave, Lord Sanderlake was sitting with the telephone to his ear. "Gordon Keble-Keith?" he murmured, and tried desperately to recall in what connection he'd heard the name. "I don't think I know you, do I?"

"Possibly not," said Keble-Keith, "but I've no doubt that you've heard of Major Stewart McQuoid?"

"Yes, I've heard of him."

"Well, in a sense, you could describe me as the man behind McQuoid," said Keble-Keith, and Lord Sanderlake's scalp tightened.

"Oh, yes," he said, in a flat voice that gave nothing away.

"To be blunt, I am the managing director of the Anglo-Antigean Development Corporation and I feel that the time has come for you and me to have a little talk."

"Do you? But what about?"

"Well——" said Keble-Keith, then broke off with a laugh. "Anyway, Lord Sanderlake, may I come and see you?"

The newspaper-proprietor hesitated, then told himself that he'd better find out just what this joker was up to. "All right," he grunted. "Come round right away, if you like."

He hung up the receiver morosely and sat for some minutes biting his nails. It was clear that something had leaked and he told himself savagely that it was his own stupid fault. "I was a fool to wait," he muttered.

"I ought to have printed the news just as soon as we established communication. I ought to have known something like this would happen."

Fifteen minutes later the dictograph on his desk crackled and informed him that a Mr. Keble-Keith was asking to see him. "He says he has an appointment," said the dictograph.

"Yes, he has. Have him shown up."

No two men could have been in greater contrast than Lord Sanderlake and Gordon Keble-Keith, and yet they took to each other at first sight. Lord Sanderlake eyed Keble-Keith's lanky figure and careless clothes and thought, "I can do business with this fellow," and Keble-Keith gazed across the desk at Lord Sanderlake's chunky torso and Napoleonic features and told himself that here was a man after his own heart.

The newspaper-proprietor offered his visitor a cigar and, when it was refused, stuck it into his own mouth. "Well, Mr. Keble-Keith, what brings you here? I was under the impression that Antigeos was a dead duck and had been for the last five years."

Keble-Keith smiled gently and remarked that since he had raised the matter he felt it behoved him to put his cards on the table. "The fact is," he said, "I happen to know that Antigeos isn't nearly such a dead duck as it seemed. To be frank, I happen to know that you and Professor Pollenport are in communication with each other."

"Oh yes? And how can you know such an extraordinary thing?"

Keble-Keith hesitated, then observed that when men carried on conversations across two hundred million miles of space they were liable to be overheard. "You see, it so chances that radio-astronomy is something of a hobby of mine," he said, "and a few nights ago I had the good fortune to pick up a message emanating from you and clearly intended for Professor Pollenport on Antigeos."

"You personally picked this up?" asked Lord Sanderlake.

"Yes. I, personally."

"And no one else knows about it?"

"No one."

"Good. But carry on."

"Well, that's about all I have to tell you," said Keble-Keith. "Unfortunately, my receiving apparatus isn't sufficiently powerful to pick up Pollenport's replies to your messages, but naturally I'm interested. After all, as you no doubt appreciate, the Corporation of which I am the managing director virtually owns Antigeos."

Lord Sanderlake jerked upright as if someone had stuck a pin into him, then threw back his head and laughed until he was breathless. "Owns it?" he gasped. "How do you make that out?"

"Stewart McQuoid's instructions were precise——"

"He's dead, by the way," put in Lord Sanderlake, quickly.

"Is he? Still, that makes no difference. His instructions, as I say, were sufficiently precise and I have no doubt he fulfilled them. He was to annex the planet formally on behalf of the Crown, and then the Corporation in its turn was to petition the Crown for the grant of a charter, which, in the circumstances, would hardly be refused."

"Wouldn't it?" muttered Lord Sanderlake.

"I think not," said Keble-Keith. "After all, there are precedents, you know—numerous ones, and all of them quite clear and unambiguous. Admittedly, no whole planet has ever been annexed before, but *terra incognita* is *terra incognita* no matter where it's found, and our legal advisers assure us that the procedure for annexing undiscovered territory is not affected by the size of the said territory. That being so, the Corporation's next step will be to proclaim the annexation."

Lord Sanderlake looked disconcerted. "What, right away?"

"Well, just as soon as possible," Keble-Keith told him. "That's to say, just as soon as the Corporation has built a transmitter sufficiently powerful to——"

"But there's no need for that!" said Lord Sanderlake hurriedly. "As you know, I'm already operating such a transmitter and I can't see that our interests conflict. So, Keble-Keith, let's get together on this thing."

The financier smiled his shark's smile, and shrugged. "Tell me, Lord Sanderlake," he said, "why haven't you already printed the news?"

"What, and let every other newspaper in on it? Oh, I know I'm taking the biggest chance of my whole career, but if I put out the story now, just what would happen? I should have boom sales for just about three issues and by then the entire gang would have climbed on to the band-wagon. No, as I see it, the most important consideration of all is that the news doesn't leak out prematurely."

"That may be a consideration from your point of view," said Keble-Keith, "but it isn't from mine. Personally, I don't care how soon the news leaks out. Right now, I've got a dormant Corporation on my hands—a Corporation whose entire capital is locked up in this venture—but from the moment the news of Antigeos hits the headlines its shares will rocket. And I'm one of the largest shareholders."

Lord Sanderlake chewed his cigar in silence for some moments, then jumped up and started pacing the room.

There was no doubt about the degree of his agitation and Keble-Keith's heart sang within him.

"In any case," he asked, "just what are you waiting for? I mean, just what eventuality are you expecting that will justify breaking the news?"

"None of your business," muttered Lord Sanderlake, but the question in itself gave him an idea of how matters might be handled, and after a few seconds' more pacing he came to Keble-Keith's chair and stood over him.

"I'll tell you what I'll do," he said: "I'll give you every scrap of information in my possession regarding Antigeos in return for your continued silence."

"My continued silence?" echoed Keble-Keith. "That sounds extremely indefinite."

"Give me six months!" cried the newspaper-proprietor. "I may not need nearly so long, but give me six months and then you can do as you like. Is it a deal?"

Keble-Keith grinned inwardly, but for the look of the thing he kept silent for the best part of a minute before he nodded and said: "All right. Yes, Lord Sanderlake, it's a deal."

Lord Sanderlake grunted and, returning to his chair, sat down heavily. . . .

IV

Both men forgot to have dinner that night. Instead, they fed on dreams of Antigeos and smoked incessantly. Keble-Keith was a man of fiercer imagination than Lord Sanderlake and now his visions of an empire in space went to the newspaper magnate's head like wine. Until that evening Lord Sanderlake had thought of Antigeos primarily as news, as the greatest scoop of all time, but Keble-Keith had a talent for inspiring people with his own grandiose conceptions—he was, after all, among other things, a company promoter—and before the evening was so very old Lord Sanderlake was seeing himself as a figure of romance, as one who went forth conquering and to conquer.

The session began with Lord Sanderlake telling his visitor of everything that he had learned from Pollenport, of the journey through space, of the landing on Antigeos's northern continent, and of the nature of that continent's inhabitants. "The Antigeosians seem to be remarkably like us in a lot of ways," said Lord Sanderlake, "but of course they are not human beings, and never will be."

Keble-Keith seemed relieved to hear it. "Half men and half monkeys, are they?" he suggested, and Lord Sanderlake had to admit that that was not his impression.

"From what Pollenport tells me," he said, "they seem to be almost as civilised as we are, and highly intelligent. In other ways, however, they don't resemble us in the least. For instance, they don't know anything about war. What's more, they've got an extra sense."

"An extra sense?" echoed Keble-Keith. "But that's impossible! What sense can a living creature have apart from the usual five?"

"I gather it's a sort of sense of movement. It seems that they have a couple of antennæ on their foreheads and, by means of them, they can sense movement without actually seeing it. And, according to Pollenport, their language is a matter of hand-movements—gestures—picked up by those extra organs, so that in fact they haven't a spoken language at all."

"H'm. Sounds like a traveller's tale to me, but carry

51

on. For instance, how primitive are they? Still at the bow-and-arrow stage, I suppose?"

"Well, hardly," said Lord Sanderlake. "No, they're a bit beyond that. It's true that they haven't got aeroplanes, but that apparently is simply because they don't like the idea of them. Yet when three or four years ago Pollenport decided to have a shot at getting back to the Earth in the old *Skylark,* they were perfectly well able to build him a booster-rocket to Sam Spencross's specification."

Keble-Keith's eyes opened wide. "What do you mean?" he asked. "They actually tried to build a spaceship?"

"I gather so, although as a matter of fact it wasn't a success. It blew up in mid-air, but at least they knew enough to build it."

"It blew up in mid-air, did it? Then how was it that Pollenport and the others weren't killed?"

"Well, it was only the booster that blew up. The *Skylark* itself survived somehow or other and came down on its parachutes. In fact, that's how Pollenport came to visit the southern continent, and he found that part of Antigeos inhabited by a terrible race with a slave-economy in full swing."

Keble-Keith's interest quickened and he started to make notes. He was like a man with two brains. There was the brain that absorbed all it was told and there was the brain that planned the future, a future that Keble-Keith saw rising in front of him in a series of golden steps. He was dreaming in terms of a hundred-million-pound flotation. Whole fleets of spaceships would have to be built and then there would be the question of an expeditionary force—since, in his view, an annexation not backed by guns could never be anything more than a fiction.

Eventually Lord Sanderlake came to the end of his sketchy account of Antigeos and then he reverted to an earlier topic. "You asked me when I intended to start printing the news," he said, "and now I'm prepared to go into that. If I splashed the news now, two things would happen. One, which I've already touched upon, is that my rivals would move into the field, and the other is that the story, because it deals with things that have happened rather than with things that are happening, would die on me in about a fortnight. What I want is a story that builds up as it goes, and now something is taking place on Antigeos that may provide just the right angle."

Keble-Keith's head jerked up. "What do you mean?"

"They're building another spaceship," said Lord Sanderlake, "and they plan to visit us."

"What, to invade us!" exclaimed Keble-Keith, with his eyes shining bright. "But, my God, that's an act of war! Tell me about this spaceship."

"I was just going to," said Lord Sanderlake, somewhat testily, and then explained that the spaceship was being planned on an enormous scale.

"And Pollenport?" asked Keble-Keith. "What does he think about it?"

"Well, at first he was somewhat sceptical, but now a new note has started to creep into his bulletins, a note of enthusiasm. In fact, both he and Spencross are beginning to think that this vast spaceship may actually make the voyage. If so, it's just the gimmick I want. The day Pollenport tells me that the ship has successfully passed its tests I shall go into action. What's more, I intend to obtain from Pollenport exclusive rights to his story of the return journey, which, incidentally, will only take a few days."

"Days!" cried Keble-Keith. "But the journey out took six months."

"That's true, but the Antigean concept of space-travel is a revolutionary one and, according to Spencross, their spaceship is as far in advance of the *Skylark* as a trans-atlantic liner is in advance of a coracle. You know, you must rid yourself of the idea that these jokers are just a bunch of simple savages."

"Well, it's clear that they're not simple," agreed Keble-Keith, "and no doubt we shall have to oppose them with armed force."

Lord Sanderlake looked up sharply. "No, no," he said. "There'll be no need for that. I mean, there's no suggestion that they're visiting us as anything other than friends."

"Friends?" sneered Keble-Keith. "I should have said that whether they come as friends or not rather depends on our attitude." He paused, then added impressively: "Lord Sanderlake, you have, I believe, a magnificent record as a man of Empire?"

The newspaper-proprietor smiled modestly, but there was no mistaking his gratification. "Well, the times have been against me," he said, "but, yes, I must admit to being a thorough-going, old-fashioned imperialist. And—as every reader of my newspapers knows—I'm not in the least ashamed to air my views."

"I thought not. Then surely it must have occurred to you at some time or other that Antigeos, the entire planet, could form a wonderful addition to the Empire."

"Y-yes," he admitted, doubtfully; "but we have to face the fact that imperialism is an unpopular doctrine——"

Keble-Keith interrupted him with a wave of his hand. "Not necessarily so," he said. "Not, for instance, when it's directed towards a planet that lacks a human population. As I see it, it's a matter of presentation."

"Presentation?" muttered Lord Sanderlake.

"Yes. If we present the Antigeosians as friendly, amenable beings we shall be defeating our own ends, shan't we? My own feeling is that they should be shown up as enemies, and savage men, from the start."

Lord Sanderlake drew a deep breath. "Difficult," he murmured. "And, I should have thought, unethical."

Keble-Keith begged to differ. "Since our ultimate intention is to introduce the glories of our civilisation to the Antigeosians," he said, "I can't see that the ethics of the matter can be anything but sound. As for the difficulties, if we go about the business in the right way, they hardly exist."

"They don't?"

"Well, no, because the point is that these people are visiting us in force, without invitation, and if that doesn't constitute an invasion, I don't know what does. Moreover—and we have Pollenport's word for it—these creatures maintain a slave-economy of a peculiarly cruel and heartless kind, and, for all we know, their invasion of the Earth has as its object the enslavement of our population."

"Just a moment," said Lord Sanderlake. "Aren't you a little confused? It's the southern Antigeosians who——"

Keble-Keith virtually ignored the interruption. "The general public," he went on, in level tones, "will know nothing more about Antigeos than the *Daily Messenger* chooses to tell them. That surely, Lord Sanderlake, must strike you as significant. I foresee a future when historians will speak of Sanderlake of Antigeos just as now they speak of Clive of India and Rhodes of Africa. You have it in your power to save the British Empire from extinction and I cannot believe you will ignore the opportunity."

Suddenly Lord Sanderlake realised that this was the moment for which his whole life had been lived and, as befitted the occasion, he stood up. "You're right!" he cried. "By God, you're right! You mean, I take it, that since the Antigeosians have seen fit to declare war upon us, we should be justified in meeting force with force, repelling the invasion, and then, in the fullness of time, carrying the war into the enemies' camp?"

"Exactly," murmured Keble-Keith.

"Very well. Then now let's get down to it and plan the campaign in detail."

Lord Sanderlake went across to a wall-safe and unlocked it. He took from it his copy of Pollenport's bulletins and brought them to the desk. The bulletins had been typed out by Digby Cox and not even Lord Sanderlake's secretary had so much as seen them. . . .

For hours the two men crouched over the desk, planning and discussing and deciding, and it wasn't until a raucous electric bell rang somewhere in the building that Lord Sanderlake at last straightened himself and leant back in his chair. The bell gave warning that the *Daily Messenger's* first edition was going to bed and Lord Sanderlake automatically glanced at his watch, which told him that the time was just past eleven.

"Well, there's no doubt about it," he said. "We've made wonderful headway, and thank God for the chance that led you to pick up my message. Ah, there's most truly a divinity that shapes our ends!"

The one quotation put him in mind of another and Keble-Keith was amused to hear the newspaper proprietor murmur something about there being a tide in the affairs of men that, taken at the flood, led on to fortune. He wondered if Lord Sanderlake would have been so pleased with the lines had he remembered that they had first been spoken by Brutus just before he marched off to death and disaster at Philippi.

Lord Sanderlake lit his sixth cigar of the evening and remarked there was one other small point. "This corporation of yours," he said. "I take it that in the circumstances the shares stand pretty low?"

Keble-Keith's heart gave a little leap and he grinned inwardly. "On the contrary," he murmured. "I can't quote you off-hand, but the last time I inquired they were still well above par. You see, the majority of the shares have got into the hands of far-sighted, enormously wealthy men—South Americans, many of them—who realise that interplanetary development isn't a matter of small profits and quick returns. Five years in their sight are as an evening gone, and I don't think you'll find that any of them are particularly anxious to unload."

Lord Sanderlake looked disappointed and muttered something about getting his broker to inquire. "Or, since we're in this thing together," he said, "I don't suppose you'd care to sell me part of your holding?"

Keble-Keith smiled and shook his head. "No," he said, "but I don't mind seeing what I can do for you in other directions. As I say, I don't know just how the market stands and the truth is that since I picked up your message I've been so taken up with the widest aspects of the matter that I haven't had time to consider it in terms of immediate profit and loss. Whatever else I may be, Lord Sanderlake, I'm not a money-grubber."

On that note, he left the newspaper-proprietor and his first task on emerging into Fleet Street was to find a telephone-box.

He rang Stanley Dutton at his home and the stock-broker grumbled at being disturbed. "I was counting on an early night," he muttered, "and now what?"

Keble-Keith asked him how he had made out. "You know, as regards Anglo-Antigean."

"Oh, that," grunted Dutton. "No difficulty at all, and by the time the market closed I had options on over ninety per cent of the stock at an average of threepence a share."

"Excellent," said Keble-Keith, then lowered his voice to observe that the price from now on was sixty shillings a share. "Do you get that, Stan—three pounds a share."

The stockbroker laughed mirthlessly. "I got it all right, but who's going to buy at that price?"

"Someone," Keble-Keith told him. "And another point is that I don't want to unload more than about half the stock. I intend to hold the rest for a rainy day."

"I'd sooner hold an umbrella," said the broker, "and if you've really got a mug who'll pay sixty bob a share I suggest you unload the lot before he's locked up. That's my advice and you can take it or leave it."

"Thanks, Stan, I'll leave it," said Keble-Keith and, as he replaced the receiver, he suddenly realised how hungry he was.

There was a snack-bar within a few doors of the telephone-box and he made his way through the fog towards it. He went in and ordered sausages-and-mashed, and a cup of tea—a modest meal for a man whose capital had just appreciated by a quarter of a million pounds. . . .

CHAPTER IV

I

FOR reasons at first not clear the news that Pollenport had established communication with the Earth had an electrifying effect upon the Antigeosians. Almost overnight the picture changed and all apathy in regard to the building of the spaceship abruptly dispersed.

Until then the construction of the enormous machine had been largely the concern of a few score enthusiasts, planning, designing and working in their own time, but within a week of the receipt of Sanderlake's first message the whole project was put on a different footing. Swarms of grey-clad workers arrived on the site and arc-lamps were introduced so that they could work by night as well as by day, and Pollenport knew enough about the organisation of Antigean society to realise that this could only mean that the highest councils were now interesting themselves in the scheme.

Even so, it was left to his oldest Antigeosian friends, Quince and Regan, to explain to him the precise reason for the change of heart.

"The whole of our community is alarmed," Quince told him. "Frankly, we do not trust the inhabitants of your Earth and, now that they know for a certainty of the existence of Antigeos, is it not likely that they will make plans to visit us in force? Perhaps even with the idea of conquering and enslaving us? Am I not right?"

"Possibly," admitted Pollenport, with a touch of sadness. "But, damn it all, your people knew that I was building a transmitter. We asked for the materials and they were supplied without a murmur. If co-operation had been denied us we couldn't have moved a finger."

"I know," agreed Quince, "but all that happened, not on an administrative level, but on an organisational one. It is the usage of our society to grant a man what he needs. When you asked for electrical equipment, perhaps the managers of the supply depots should have queried the request, but the fact is they didn't. Consequently, the Councils of Elders knew nothing about the transmitter until they heard the news that messages had been received from the Earth and by then, of course, it was too late."

Pollenport asked how it was he was still allowed to go on transmitting messages and receiving them. "No one has even suggested to me that I ought to stop," he said.

Regan smiled and touched his hand affectionately. "But why should you stop?" she asked. "We know you, Professor Pollenport, and we trust you. And we love you. We know that whatever you tell your people about us will be the truth."

Pollenport blushed faintly and thanked her. "In any case," he remarked, "there's no immediate danger. In the first place, old Sanderlake, for reasons of policy, is keeping the news to himself for the time being, and, in the second place, the building of spaceships takes time. I shall be very surprised if anyone from the Earth succeeds in visiting Antigeos within three years, and as for an invasion by force, why, it would take at least ten, and more likely twenty."

Quince looked doubtful. "You may be right, Professor," he said, "but even so, our concern is to establish good relations with your people just as quickly as possible. From all that you have told us, the inhabitants of the Earth are very suggestible, and if once they start looking upon us as enemies, it will be a disastrous thing—both for our planet and for yours." He paused, then added: "And, you know, we haven't forgotten Stewart McQuoid."

"No," said Pollenport, "but for Heaven's sake don't think of my people as ravening beasts. The vast majority of human beings are decent and good-hearted, and no more like Stewart McQuoid than I am. They aren't villains."

"You tell me that," murmured Quince, "yet throughout your history you seem to have done little except kill and torture each other. It is very strange. . . ."

II

The Antigeosians' spaceship was so unlike any spaceship that Sam Spencross had ever conceived that, as he often remarked, he did not know what to make of it. He spent every waking hour on the construction site, breathing the dusty air and sweating in the torrid heat, and tried to make up his mind as to whether the immense machine would ever ascend into space or not.

He knew now the principles upon which the spaceship was designed and, while he was intrigued by them, he was far from being convinced of their practicability; and, in fact, he said as much to Timothy Penn one breathless afternoon when they were lying in the shade of some rocks watching a team of grey-clad workers struggling with a helicopter unit that was being hoisted towards the spaceship's outer rim.

"I'll admit that they've gone into the theory of space-travel with extraordinary thoroughness," he said, "and, of course, they learned a lot when they built us that

61

booster-rocket, but whether they really know what they're up to I'm damned if I can say. They seem to have got hold of some rummy ideas, to me."

"But what exactly are their ideas?"

"Topsy-turvy ones," said Sam, grinning, "but they argue that it's us who have got hold of the wrong end of the stick. They say that we've misled ourselves by working too closely to the analogy of the ordinary rocket, and they maintain that what is needed in the early stages of the flight, when you have the atmosphere to contend with, isn't a powerful boosting force, but a steady lifting one. And hence the helicopters. That helicopter unit they're hoisting now is only the first of three hundred and they're going to be spaced all the way round the outer rim at intervals of about ten feet. Their job is to lift the whole contraption gently from the ground until a height of fifteen thousand feet is reached, and at that point the jet-propulsion units take over. There are going to be two hundred of them, fixed to the inner ring, and it's planned that they'll lift the ship to about sixty thousand feet. And at that height the reaction-propulsion units come into play and they're built into the body of the spaceship itself. In fact, the only thing we really agree about is that, once out in space, reaction-propulsion is the only possible motive-force."

"Still, there's quite a lot to be said for their plan, isn't there?" asked Timothy. "I mean, we shan't suffer as much as we suffered on the *Skylark* from the rate of acceleration, shall we?"

"Presumably not," agreed Sam. "Naturally, the spaceship will be subjected to a steady acceleration from the moment it leaves the ground, but nothing resembling escape-velocity will be reached until the ship is an immense distance from the plane — two or three hundred miles at least. Now that's all very well in theory, but will it work out in practice?"

"Well, will it?"

Sam wiped the beads of sweat from his forehead and shrugged. "It's a problem of mass-ratio," he said, "and the trouble is that neither Jonah nor I can understand Antigean mathematics. I suppose they've got it right, but it seems a shaky do to me. And, Timothy, the fuel they're using! Why, it would have kept the old *Skylark* running for a lifetime."

"What sort of fuel?"

"Monatomic hydrogen," said Sam. "The same as us, and you can't beat it. They're planning to carry enough to make the return journey too, and what there won't be much of is food. They argue that we shan't need much in the way of stores, because we shall only be in space for about a fortnight."

"Good Lord, then we shall be travelling almost at the speed of light, shan't we?"

Sam laughed. "Hardly," he said. "If we could travel at the speed of light, we should be home in twenty minutes, but even if we spend a fortnight on the journey we shan't be loitering. The spaceship's course will cut right across the terrestrial orbit, and we shall only miss the sun by about forty million miles. In fact, for the first half of the journey, the Antigeosians reckon to use the sun's gravitational pull to help us on our way and, for the second half, as a braking agent. From the moment we leave Antigeos acceleration is continuous until the half-way mark is reached, and, from then on, deceleration is continuous until we finally touch down on the Earth."

Timothy was just about to ask another question when Paul Greenwod appeared. He drifted towards them from the direction of the little railway, and greeted them languidly. "Hullo, you two," he drawled. "I've brought you some news."

He threw himself down on the sand and remarked that it was hot.

"Certainly it's hot," said Timothy; "but what's your news?"

Paul scooped up a handful of the dark sand and let it trickle through his fingers. "Prospero wants to see Jonah," he murmured.

"Prospero?" exclaimed Timothy. "But I thought no one ever saw him!"

"Well, Jonah's going to. The news that Prospero wanted to see him came through on the disseminator about half an hour ago, and Jonah set off right away."

"Alone?"

"Uh-huh. Regan and Quince have gone with him to interpret, and I grabbed a rail-car and came over here to tell you."

"But Prospero lives miles away, doesn't he?"

"That's right," said Paul. "Way over on the other side of the great lake—nearly a thousand miles from here. Oh, I guess we shan't see anything of Jonah for a week or so."

"I wonder what it's all about!"

"Who knows?" muttered Paul, and rolled over on to his back. "Maybe Prospero just wants to see what a human being looks like. . . . Gee, they sure are getting ahead with that spaceship, and what a big bang it'll make when it blows up!"

It was, of course, the humans who had christened him Prospero, following their custom of giving their hosts Shakespearean names, but none of them had ever met him. On the other hand, it would have been impossible for them not to have heard of him, for he was easily the most famous of living Antigeosians. His reputation rested primarily on a number of historical and philosophical works that he had written in his middle age, and his prestige was enormous.

Pollenport, who had long ago mastered the Antigean written language, had read many of Prospero's writings, and he had been somewhat piqued when his attempts to meet the sage were scotched.

"He lives in a very distant part," Quince had told him, when he first suggested a meeting. "He lives in the north, beyond the great lake."

"Well, that's only a thousand miles or so. We could make it in a few days."

"Yes, but I still doubt if he would see you. He would say he is too old and, in these days, it's the truth that almost no one sees him except a few of the Elders who go to him to ask his advice."

"How old is he, then?"

"Nearly a hundred and ten, which is to say that if he were a human being he would be about ninety."

"Still, I'd like him to know that I want to meet him," said Pollenport. "Might I write him a letter, do you think?"

"Certainly," said Quince, and that same afternoon he helped Pollenport compose a suitable letter.

All that had happened more than two years before and Prospero's reply to Pollenport's letter had led to a regular correspondence. The sage's interest in the Earth was detailed and comprehensive, and it was clear, from the questions he posed, that he was far from being in his dotage, which made his refusal to meet Pollenport more inexplicable than ever.

"Why do you think he's suddenly changed his mind?" Pollenport asked, soon after he, accompanied by Quince and Regan, set out for Prospero's home.

"It's impossible to say," Quince told him. "But certainly the reasons for his decision are public ones, otherwise the news of the invitation would not have come over the disseminator. Probably he wants to consult your opinion of the projected space-flight."

"Well, now that I'm going to see him, can you tell me why it is that he's never agreed to meet me before?"

Quince and Regan exchanged glances, but said nothing.

"There is a particular reason, is there?" asked Pollenport.

It was Regan who answered him this time. "Yes, there is, Jonah," she said, "but we feel it is not for us to tell you. When you meet Prospero you will understand."

Pollenport let the subject drop and for some time the three of them travelled in silence, a silence that was broken only by the gentle purring of the rail-car's wheels along the track. They sped past the great geyser that marked the limits of the Land of Fountains, and then for a spell they traversed a monotonously lush landscape of rolling pasture-lands. Towards evening the scenery changed again and they found themselves travelling across arable land brilliant with the great circular flower-fields that were such a feature of the Antigean scene. Quince gestured towards the glowing landscape with a sweep of his arm and remarked that he

66

supposed it made Pollenport happy to think that he would soon be leaving it all behind.

Pollenport laughed and drew down the corners of his mouth. "If you'd asked me that a few weeks ago," he said, "I'd have replied with an unqualified 'yes', but now—well, I don't know. In fact, I'm inclined to think that if I had only myself to consider I'd be quite happy to end my days here."

"Why?" asked Regan.

"Well, I've been remote from the Earth's hurly-burly for so long," Pollenport told her, "that now I feel somewhat reluctant to return to it. I'd forgotten what it was like until I found myself in communication with old Sanderlake again."

He grinned ruefully and added that only that morning he had had another batch of messages from the old brigand. "And from the tone of them," he said, "one would think that the Almighty called Antigeos into being solely for the benefit of the *Daily Messenger's* circulation. He wants to know when we're setting off, why can't I give him an approximate date of departure and whether I'll sell him exclusive rights to all the material connected with the expedition."

Regan frowned. "I don't understand," she murmured. "What are 'exclusive rights'?"

Pollenport tried to explain, but soon gave it up as hopeless. "Anyway, it's not worth troubling your head about," he told her; "but there's one thing I can guarantee and that is that as soon as you arrive on the Earth you'll be signed up to dictate a series of articles on 'The Antigean woman's angle'. I'm warning you!"

In all, the journey took four days and they spent the first night in the rail-car, travelling all night and taking it in turns to sleep on the rail-car's cushioned seats. After that, however, they ran into wet weather and so

67

spent the second and third nights at habitations. There was a letter awaiting Quince at the second of these habitations. It was from Prospero, but Quince did not divulge its contents to Pollenport until some time after they had started on the last lap of the journey.

The morning was clear and bright, and the air, washed by the rain of the two previous days, seemed to sparkle in the sunshine. The chalklands they were passing over were flat and uninteresting, but Regan remarked to Pollenport that soon they would come to the great lake, the vast inland sea that Pollenport had never visited. "We shall skirt its southern shore," she said, "and then, in the early afternoon, we shall arrive at Prospero's home."

It was then that Quince told Pollenport about the letter he had received from Prospero, and he seemed faintly embarrassed. "It was not a long letter," he said, "but in it he asked me to explain to you why he has never agreed to meet you before."

"Oh yes?"

"Well, the truth is that he is very badly crippled."

"I'm sorry to hear that," murmured Pollenport, "but he shouldn't have let it deter him from meeting me. As you know, we humans are more used to confronting illness and affliction than you are."

Yet, now that the matter had been explained to him, he understood Prospero's reluctance. The Antigeosians had an almost Erewhonian attitude to physical disabilities. Each of them felt that he owed it not merely to himself but to the community as a whole to keep as fit as possible, and illness was not something that could be talked about without shame.

"In the past," said Quince, "Prospero was very fond of mountaineering, and he continued to climb mountains when he was really too old for it. Then, about twenty years ago, he was terribly injured by a fall of rock. His body was crushed, and both legs and an arm had to be amputated." He hesitated, then added, "He has asked me to apologise to you in advance for any tediousness that may result from your interview. You see, with only one hand . . ."

Quince let his sentence trail off into silence, but Pollenport understood what he was getting at. Clearly, since Prospero had only one hand, it would be difficult for him to express himself in the gesture-language, and it was possible, even, that he would have to write everything down.

IV

The habitation in which Prospero lived was so small as to be little more than a private dwelling for the great man and his disciples. It had been hewn into the white cliff-face on the shore of the lake, and rail-cars entered it through a tunnel at the foot of the cliff. There were no roller-esplanades and the bathing-hall was no larger than a fair-sized English drawing-room. The inhabitants were for the most part ascetic-looking and elderly, and there was about the habitation a simplicity and lack of luxury that contrasted strikingly with the busy and colourful habitations of the south.

The visitors were greeted by a woman with white hair who had a little English. She was by no means young, but she had a fine presence and carried herself erect, and it occurred to Pollenport that in her youth she must have been quite astoundingly beautiful.

She accompanied them towards the bathing-hall and on the way explained to Pollenport that she had been

Prospero's companion for many years. "On the Earth you would say husband and wife," she told him. "We have two sons and a daughter."

Pollenport decided to call her Imogen, and when he, Quince and Regan had bathed and changed, she suggested that he would probably like to meet Prospero right away. "I expect you hungry," she said. "But will be fruit and wine there, and afterwards you have a meal."

She led them along broad corridors until presently they came to the doorway of a small blue-and-white room, which overlooked the lake from a wide window set in the face of the cliff. Prospero's couch was by the window and the blue rug that was loosely wrapped round him concealed everything except his head and one arm. He did not look so extraordinarily old. His broad, intelligent face was unlined, except by two deep creases, one on each side of his mouth, and his eyes, when they fell on Pollenport, lit up in a curiously youthful way. He was completely bald, however, which was unusual for an Antigeosian, and his baldness had the effect of making his antennæ exceptionally noticeable.

He greeted Pollenport with a warm smile, and said: "I speak no English except these few words, but— welcome, Professor Pollenport!"

He held out his one hand and Pollenport grasped it, while Quince replied to the sage's greeting in the gesture-language. Chairs were brought up and each of the visitors accepted fruit from a bowl that Imogen handed round.

Graceful flame-coloured birds as large as albatrosses were swooping and diving above the lake and Prospero waved towards them and glanced at Imogen, who explained that the birds were peculiar to that part of

70

Antigeos. She wanted to add something more, but her English was not up to it, so Quince helped out.

"She says that Prospero spends much time watching the birds," he told Pollenport, "and meditating on their ways."

The interview was technically a difficult one, in that Prospero, having but one hand, used a form of the gesture-language that only Imogen of those present could understand. Consequently, she had to translate everything that he said to Quince, who in turn put it into English.

"Prospero apologises," said Quince, "and observes that now you will no doubt understand why it is that he has never before put you to this inconvenience. Now that you are returning to the Earth, however, he feels that the importance of the occasion overrides all other considerations, particularly as there are several points he wants to take up with you."

First, there was the question of establishing friendly relations between the two planets. "We want you, Professor Pollenport," said Prospero, "to convey messages of goodwill to your people. However, on Antigeos, as you know, we have no king or president—or indeed any head of state whatsoever—and so the question arose as to who should sign the messages. The leading Councils of Elders have conferred on the matter with the result that I have been invited to act, as far as relations with the Earth are concerned, as president. The honour is totally undeserved, but nevertheless I have accepted and now I am going to request your assistance. Will you stay here two or three days and help me in the drafting of the messages?"

"Well, my knowledge of protocol is extremely limited," said Pollenport, with a smile, "but I'll do my best. The first thing I should like to know is whereabouts upon the Earth you plan to land the spaceship?"

When the question had been translated, Prospero said that that was one of the things he wished to discuss. "Which of the terrestrial areas would you favour, Professor Pollenport?" he asked.

"England," said Pollenport, promptly. "For one thing, it is my own country, for another, there would be no language difficulty and, for a third, I have already, as you know, established communication with people in England. On the other hand, your engineers may feel that the technical difficulties of landing on such a small and congested island will be too great."

Prospero asked if there were no sparsely populated areas in England, and Pollenport mentioned Dartmoor and Salisbury Plain. "Of the two, Salisbury Plain would probably be better," he said. "It's more or less in the centre of England, and it's nearer London than Dartmoor."

Some discussion of the idea followed, and terrestrial maps, reproduced from atlases that had once formed part of the *Skylark*'s library, were brought in. Until then, it seemed, Prospero had been in favour of a landing on one of the great continental areas, where there would be no risk of falling into the sea, but eventually he came round to Pollenport's point of view and promised to forward the suggestion to the appropriate council, endorsing it with his recommendation. "At least our engineers will probably accept it," he said, as interpreted by Quince, "since it's always been their claim that they could land the spaceship within a thousand paces of any given spot."

Another factor that was bothering Prospero was the temper of the English natives. "We get the impression," he said, "from such histories as have been translated into our language, that your people are exceptionally fierce

72

and bloodthirsty. After all, your nation has at one time or another subjugated more than a quarter of the Earth to its rule, and we cannot think that that was achieved solely by kindness——"

"No, it wasn't," Pollenport put in, "and I must admit that when it comes to predacity we have a record unequalled by any nation since the Romans, but that isn't to say that you have anything to fear from us. I shall be carrying messages of friendship from you and I think you can rest assured that they'll be honoured."

Prospero stirred uneasily on his couch and gazed out across the lake. There was already more than a hint of evening in the air and the big birds no longer flew above the lake, but had settled on the water with their heads hidden under their wings. More than a minute passed before Prospero at last looked back into the room, and then he addressed Imogen in slow, carefully-considered gestures. His remarks appeared to worry her a little and when she conveyed their import to Quince he too seemed disturbed, and was hesitant about his translation as if he expected Pollenport to take offence.

He said: "Prospero begs you to forgive the question, but he wants to know if there is any risk of your people firing their guns at the spaceship as it lands—before, that is to say, any messages of goodwill can be delivered."

"Most unlikely," said Pollenport. "Public opinion would not allow it, and you must remember that the people, collectively, are almost always more decent than the politicians who profess to lead them. By the time the spaceship lands everyone will be expecting it, thanks to Lord Sanderlake, and in my despatches I shall emphasise your friendly intentions."

Prospero's next question concerned Lord Sanderlake. "Do you trust him?" was the import of it.

73

Pollenport laughed and said that he only trusted him in certain directions. "You can't trust a lion not to bite you," he said, "but you can trust it not to kick you, and that's rather how Sanderlake is. It wouldn't increase his newspaper's circulation to suppress the news of your pacific intentions, and so I think we can trust him not to do it."

Prospero continued to look uneasy and, in a series of rapid and incisive gestures, indicated that he wished someone more responsible than Sanderlake were picking up Pollenport's transmissions. "In your last letter," he said, "you told me that so far Sanderlake has not printed a word about Antigeos in his newspaper. Why is that?"

"Sheer greed," said Pollenport. "His lifelong ambition has been to boost the sales of the *Daily Messenger* to ten million, and if he printed the news prematurely all the other newspapers would hurriedly build transmitters and start searching the ether until they found the right wave-length. Naturally, we're putting out signals on all sorts of wave-lengths, in the hope of making contact with someone else, but, as we're limited to the ultra-short band, the chances of its happening are slender."

Prospero closed his eyes and pursed his lips, and his next remark, as translated by Quince, was: "What an extraordinary place the Earth must be! One man has a petty ambition and to further it two thousand million people are kept in ignorance. . . . But what happens to him when your Government finds out what he has done?"

"Nothing," said Pollenport. "Nothing can happen to him."

It was growing dark. Beyond the lake the sun was setting redly, and now the ceiling of the little room

74

started to glow with clear white light as someone somewhere touched a switch.

Prospero opened his eyes, and asked Pollenport if he had arranged for his radio equipment to be installed in the spaceship.

"Yes. I've discussed it with the engineers and we've so organised it that the whole lot can be shifted within a matter of hours."

When this had been translated, Prospero nodded and gave Pollenport a pleased smile, and his next remark was so startling that it took Pollenport's breath away. In fact, he could not believe his ears when he heard Quince say that the spaceship was due to take off in eight days' time.

"How's that again, Quince?" he asked. "Eight days? Surely you must mean eighty?"

Quince queried the statement, but it seemed that there had been no mistake, and Pollenport gave a surprised laugh.

"Well, that's wonderful!" he exclaimed. "But why the sudden hurry?"

Apparently, it was all on account of Mercury. "As you know," said Prospero, via Imogen and Quince, "it is planned to pass within about forty million miles of the sun and the idea is to use Mercury as a sort of parasol. You will travel in Mercury's shadow, and if you missed the present transit it would mean waiting another whole quarter-year!"

v

Before dawn, Regan slipped noiselessly into Timothy's and Rose's sleeping compartment, and

touched the button that put on the light. She woke
Rose by gently shaking her.

"It's time!" she whispered. "Wake up, Rose."

Rose opened her eyes. She frowned and blinked, as
if she couldn't make out where she was or what was
happening.

Then she remembered, and sat up, rubbing her eyes.
"Thank you, Regan," she murmured. "We'll get up
right away."

Regan left them. Timothy grumbled sleepily at being
disturbed and rolled over on to his back. "Wass
smatter?" he muttered.

"Wake up, darling. Today's the day!"

She yawned again, and then, with a sudden effort, got
to her feet. Timothy propped himself up on an elbow
and scratched his head. "Oh, let's not go," he mumbled.
"Let's just stay here and get some sleep."

It was too early for anything like a genuine smile
but Rose did her best. "Now don't fall asleep again,"
she warned him, as she left the compartment. "I'm
going to get Prue."

The whole habitation was as silent as a desert and
Rose hurried across to the children's dormitory. She
went to the compartment that Prue shared with Mab,
Puck and three or four other children, and entered it
on tiptoe. By the subdued blue light that glowed from
the compartment's ceiling she managed to sort out the
children's identities. Prue was sound asleep with her
arms round Mab and her head pillowed on Puck's chest.

Rose lifted her gently, but not so gently that Prue
didn't protest.

"No, Mummy!" she mumbled. "No, I didn't——"

Rose hushed her and hastily retreated. Prue started
to cry. "I didn't finish sleeping!" she protested, and
struggled to escape from Rose's arms.

76

"I know, precious, but don't you remember? It's today that——"

Prue's sense of injustice, however, blinded her to all other considerations and she let out a wail that echoed round the dormitories like a steam-whistle, and Rose was relieved when they ran into Timothy at the top of the spiral stairs.

"For heaven's sake, reason with your daughter," she whispered. "One more scream like that and she'll have the whole place in an uproar!"

Timothy was not impressed. "I feel like screaming myself," he muttered. "All I want to do is sleep."

He took Prue from Rose and led the way to the bathing-hall, and when they had bathed they all of them felt a shade more cheerful. They dressed, and Rose advised Timothy to put on a padded tunic over an ordinary one. "It's going to be bitter crossing the plain," she said. "I'm dressing Prue up like an Eskimo."

"What's an Eskimo?" asked Prue, sullenly.

"Please, Prue—not quite so early in the morning. Eskimos can keep till later."

Regan was waiting for them in the dining-hall, and as they sat down to a typical Antigean breakfast—honey-cakes and cream and a hot fruit-drink—Rose was haunted by feelings of nostalgia. Everything she did, she told herself she was doing for the last time, and had a messenger come to them during breakfast to tell them that the space-flight was cancelled she was inclined to think that she would have been more relieved than disappointed. Prue firmly refused to eat her honey-cake and faced the world with a brooding scowl. "I didn't finish sleeping," she muttered at intervals.

Rose was right about the morning's chilliness and, as they set out in a rail-car across the plain, they were glad of their padded tunics. The sky was a faded grey streaked with pale light in the east. The white mist lay low over the plain and the geysers and fountains, playing over it, looked ghostly and unreal.

Prue was deeply silent for the first part of the journey, then suddenly remembered Puck and Mab. "I didn't say good-bye to them," she announced stormily.

"But you did, sweetheart," said Rose. "You said good-bye to them last night."

"I didn't say good-bye to them this morning."

"No, because they were asleep. Oh, Prue, don't you remember I explained to you last night that you wouldn't be able to say good-bye to them this morning."

Prue changed the subject. "Why's it dark?" she asked.

"Because the sun isn't up yet. You see, you're up before the sun. It's fun, isn't it?"

Prue's expression suggested that it was anything but fun and a few seconds later she climbed on to Rose's lap. "I don't want to go, Mummy," she whispered, and Rose hugged her, thinking, "That makes two of us."

She said: "You'll love it once we start. It will be wonderfully exciting, much more exciting than anything else you've ever done."

Timothy glanced at Regan. "I wonder how old Jonah feels this morning," he said. "I expect we'll find that he's already started transmitting."

"Perhaps," said Regan. "But it's still very early."

Jonah, Sam and Paul had joined the spaceship overnight with the idea of getting all the radio-equipment into full going order. They had more or less been signed on as members of the crew, while Timothy and Rose were travelling as passengers, which was just as it had been on the *Skylark*.

The rail-car rattled into the tunnel and this morning Prue was too demoralised even to pretend to be brave about it. She buried her face in Rose's neck and sobbed

78

unashamedly, and clung so tightly that Rose was half-suffocated before the rail-car emerged into the twilight on the far side.

Darkness still stagnated in the valley-bottom, but there was plenty going on. The hills reverberated with the crash of metal on metal, grey-clad workers hurried hither and thither through the half-light and when Rose looked up she saw that the air-screws of the three hundred helicopters were slowly turning, silhouetted against the pale sky. An air of suspense hung over the great machine as if it had just drawn a deep breath.

Regan stopped the rail-car as it came abreast of the first pylon and Timothy swung himself over the side. He took Prue from Rose and, as he did so, the first rays of the sun struck down over the eastern hills. Prue stopped whimpering and gazed in that direction. "I was up before the sun, wasn't I?" she said, suddenly interested. . . .

VI

The start of the ascent was so gentle that Rose could not have named either this moment or that one as the moment of departure. For fifteen minutes before the actual take-off the spaceship had been trembling and vibrating, even seeming to lift and fall a little like a moored balloon, and it was not until Rose saw the head of one of the pylons move across her field of vision that she realised they were airborne.

"We've started!" she breathed, and hugged Prue to her in her excitement. The two of them, and Regan, were gazing down through a large port-hole while lying on the floor of the strange curvilinear compartment that had been allotted to them.

The throb of three hundred helicopters filled the air, and slowly Rose's field of vision grew until it included the whole length and breadth of the valley. Crowds of waving Antigeosians lined the slopes, and the spaceship's elongated shadow, thrown by the rising sun, rolled westward over them.

The green levels of the Land of Fountains crept into view and Prue, looking towards the habitation, squeaked: "I think I can see Puck and Mab! I think I can!"

The spaceship was slowly rotating and its motion brought the beaches and the coastline into sight, and in the western distance Rose could just make out the great peninsula like a mauve cloud against the sky.

Timothy came in and joined them at the port-hole, throwing himself down between Regan and Rose.

"Everything's under control," he murmured, "and I've been helping Jonah. Are you all right?"

"Of course," said Rose, although in fact she was feeling far from happy. There was something uncanny and almost sinister about the steadiness of the huge machine's ascent and she could not help remembering how much more exhilarating had been the *Skylark's* take-off. Then everything had seemed to happen at once and there had been no time for apprehension, whereas now there was plenty of time for every sort of unwelcome emotion. Besides, she was older now, and she had Prue.

Paul looked into the compartment. "Oh, swell, you're all lying down," he said, "and that's how it should be. There's a general order out to the effect that everyone's to lie down until we're out in space. In five minutes' time the jets take over."

"Is Jonah still transmitting?" asked Timothy.

"Sure, but we're not picking up any signals from the Earth. At least we haven't since the take-off, but I guess that will right itself later on."

The clouded mountains of the southern continent hove into view and directly beneath the spaceship the sea shone like smelted bronze in the reddish sunlight. Rose's fingers closed over Timothy's hand and pressed it, and at the same moment the spaceship was shaken by a series of subdued, cough-like explosions.

"The jets!" exclaimed Timothy, and Prue glanced up at Rose anxiously.

Rose smiled reassuringly and kissed her daughter's ear. "It's all right, precious," she murmured, and wished that she had even half the confidence her words expressed.

The barking and coughing of the jets levelled out, and now the spaceship was rising in earnest. Rose could feel the floor of the compartment pressing upwards against her breasts, stomach and thighs, and Prue bumped her nose against the port-hole. "It hit me, Mummy!" she said, and giggled.

Clouds enveloped the spaceship, blotting out land and sea, and now the roar of the jets was so loud that Timothy could hardly make himself heard above it. "Keep your head down, Prue," he shouted, "or you'll bump your nose again."

Prue obeyed him by resting her head on the port-hole and clinging to Rose's arm.

Rose grinned at her cheerfully. "It's fun, isn't it?" she yelled, but Prue, judging from her expression, was by no means convinced of it. She didn't take her eyes off Rose's face for a moment, and Rose could only hope that she was managing to keep her own uncertainties decently hidden.

She glanced at Timothy. "Some acceleration!" she shouted.

"Yes, but it's nothing to what we put up with on the *Skylark*!"

No doubt that was so, but the acceleration was more prolonged, and well before the spaceship emerged from the banks of cloud all the muscles of Rose's body were aching with the strain. Regan had had the sense to turn over on her back, but it was impossible for Rose, with Prue clinging to her, to follow suit and so there was nothing for it but to grin and bear it.

The clouds thinned and then suddenly the spaceship was above them. The pressure of the acceleration eased a little and Prue let go of Rose's arm. She caught a glimpse of the Antigean coastline through a gap in the clouds and her excitement and interest returned. "Mummy, haven't we gone a long way?" she screamed. "Are we nearly there?"

"Where, pet?"

"At the place you said. You know, at the place you were when you were a little girl."

"Oh, no, Prue—we shan't get there yet. We've still a long way to go."

"I don't mind," said Prue, and returned her attention to the port-hole.

Paul looked in again to ask how they were getting on. "They're just starting up the reaction-motors," he said. "Listen. . . ."

A rumble like distant thunder was just discernible beneath the roar of the jets and, as they listened, it grew louder. Rose slipped an arm round Prue and held her to her, rolling over on to her back as she did so. "Hold tight, Prue," she murmured. "There may be another bump."

There was, and it was severe enough for Rose to be glad that she was on her back. With Prue's weight pressing against her chest all the breath was squeezed from her lungs, and for some seconds she felt sick and giddy,

82

as if she were drowning. A sharp explosion like a sudden clap of thunder made her nerves jump, but immediately afterwards she heard Paul's voice, calm and reassuring.

"A back-fire in the combustion-chamber, I guess," he said. "Forget it. It's nothing."

Two more explosions shook the spaceship and then the reaction-motors steadied down to a sustained deep-throated roar, a noise that was to become so familiar to them that soon it would have only the significance of silence.

Paul had dropped to the floor as the spaceship bucked and now he scrambled to his feet. "Okay, folks," he said. "From now on it'll be a hayride, so you can get up and stretch your legs. Only steady how you go—she's heaving a bit."

"So'm I," muttered Timothy with a grin as he got up. He helped Prue to her feet and once more she asked if they were nearly there.

Timothy laughed. "No, we're not," he told her, "and before we go any further I think you'd better get it firmly fixed in your head that we shan't be there for days and days. But you'll have a lot of fun on the way. Why, soon you'll be floating about just as if you were in a swimming-pool, only more so."

Paul suggested that they all went up to the observation-gallery. "You can see more from there," he said.

VII

Imagine an ice-hockey puck, and that, except for the rings that held the jet and helicopter units, gives an idea of the spaceship's shape. Then imagine that puck magnified until it is about a thousand feet across and three thousand feet in circumference, and that gives an idea of the spaceship's size. The observation-gallery ran round the edge of this enormous puck for its whole circumference and, since its walls were transparent, one's view of the heavens from it was unrestricted.

Rose clung to the hand-rail and gazed down, feeling overawed. Timothy was at her side with Prue in his arms and he could feel Prue's heart beating like a little trip-hammer under his hand. For some minutes she gazed down at the receding planet, then looked up at him with a strained smile which told him that she was frightened even as she said she wasn't. "I'm not a tiny bit frightened," she told him. "Are you?"

"I don't think so," said Timothy. "After all, there's nothing to be frightened of."

The sky was growing dark. During the ascent it had deepened through all the shades of blue until now it was nearly indigo, pierced here and there by the albedos of stars. The Antigean horizon was now unmistakably curved, and Paul, on Rose's other side, glanced at his watch. "I guess we're nearing escape-velocity," he said. "And I can begin to feel a sort of lightness creeping over me already, can't you?"

"Yes," said Rose faintly, and she was in no mood for conversation. Fears were assailing her such as had never troubled her on the *Skylark,* and it needed all her will-power to keep them at bay. The size and efficiency of the Antigean spaceship awed her and she felt almost superstitious about it, as if the very perfection of the ascent were a challenge to fate.

Then Sam Spencross appeared. He came lurching towards them along the gallery with one hand on the hand-rail to counteract a slight tendency to float.

"Well, we've made it!" he cried, as he approached them.

"Escape-velocity?" asked Paul.

"Yes. I've just run into Horatio and he told me. Now we're out in space, or as good as!"

The spaceship's rotation had brought them round to face the sun, a white circle of cheerless fire without rays or effulgence, and the unreasoning terror that broke loose in Rose was so overwhelming that she had to close her eyes and clench her teeth to prevent herself screaming.

Timothy sensed that something was wrong. "What is it?" he murmured.

It was a struggle for her to speak. "Nothing," she gasped. "Actually I feel a little sick. I think I'll go and lie down."

"I'll come with you."

Regan undertook to look after Prue, and Timothy and Rose escaped from the sun's baleful glare into a corridor. As soon as they were out of sight of the gallery Timothy asked her again what was the matter.

She flung herself into his arms with her face against his. "I don't know, Timothy," she whispered. "I feel as if—I feel as if something awful is going to happen!"

CHAPTER V

I

IT was snowing in London and the wind was cold as ice. In Bellamina's a girl with smooth blonde hair sat by the window and watched the driving snow, and scanned the faces of the passers-by as they hurried along Coventry Street with their heads down and their chins in their collars.

She was a pretty girl with the level eyebrows and wide mouth of the innately good-tempered, and in fact she was so good-tempered that no one ever minded keeping her waiting. "Oh, Deborah'll be all right," her friends said. "Nothing ever ruffles Deborah!"

There was a sherry on the table in front of her and so far she had made it last twenty minutes. She was beginning to wonder if anything serious could have happened and, for the third time, she wiped the mist from the window's plate-glass with her glove. She wouldn't worry, she told herself, if only he hadn't been so certain that tonight he'd be dead on time. "I must be punctual on your birthday," he had said, "and there's absolutely no reason why I shouldn't finish at nine sharp. Then I'll have a quick drink with the boys and be with you at half-past."

Half-past nine—and now it was nearly ten. Every few minutes Deborah's gaze travelled to the clock above the bar, and now she began to think of all the things that might have happened. If he had been delayed at the office, he would have telephoned her. If he had been taken seriously ill, someone else would have telephoned

—unless, of course, he'd been seized with amnesia, or something like that.

She dismissed that possibility as being fantastic, and then thought, "A car smash?"

She glanced out uneasily at the cars and taxis slithering past, and tried to rid herself of the idea. Surely even Jim wouldn't be such a goop as to bring the car out on a night like this? It was an open car, ancient and powerful, and with the roads covered in half-frozen slush it would be asking for trouble.

The waiters were starting to look at her askance (or perhaps she only imagined it), and at last her noted good temper started to show signs of strain. Jim might be endearingly scatter-brained, but even he should realise that Bellamina's lounge wasn't the sort of place where a girl could sit indefinitely.

She took her cigarette-case out of her bag and came to a decision. She would smoke just one cigarette, and if he hadn't turned up by when it was finished, she would leave.

She lit the cigarette and was just shaking out the match when the swing-door swung open and there he was, with a shamefaced grin and a very red nose from the cold. He took off his hat and shook the snow from it as he crossed the lounge, then hurriedly produced a small package from an inner pocket.

"The present!" he exclaimed, putting the package into her hand and kissing her. "And many happy returns of the day, but please don't thank me, because I embarrass so easily. . . . It's a watch, as if you didn't know."

She smiled happily and, while she unwrapped the watch, Jim ordered two sherries. "Though God knows what I want a sherry for," he remarked. "I'm as hungry as a hyena already."

"Are hyenas particularly hungry?"

"Of course, and that's what they howl about."

The watch was a success and Deborah's eyes shone with pleasure as she slipped it on to her wrist. "Jim, you're a pet," she murmured, "and now all the girls at the office will be simply mad with envy." She compared the watch with the clock above the bar. "It's the right time, too."

"Yes, I know," sighed Jim, "and I don't suppose there's another man in town dumb enough to give a girl a watch when he's half an hour late. Still, you've only to hear what I'm going to tell you when all will be forgiven. Maybe."

"What do you mean?" she asked, but before he could reply the waiter arrived with the sherries.

Jim was five years older than Deborah, which made him twenty-five, and he was as dark as she was fair. His face was long, thin and humorous and no one had ever yet known him to wear the same expression for ten seconds together. He was a newspaperman by calling, his paper was the *Daily Post,* and so far his career was remarkable more for the enthusiasm he brought to it than for any success it brought to him.

The waiter departed and Jim became confidential. "Don't breathe a word of this," he whispered, "but I think I'm on to something tremendous. An angle, that's all I want—an angle! All day long Fleet Street's been buzzing with rumours and the general idea is that the *Daily Messenger's* gone mad!"

"Darling, take it a little more slowly. I don't think you're making sense."

"But, Deborah, it has gone mad," he assured her, "and my own theory is that Lord Sanderlake has suddenly turned radio-active or something, and so they've locked all the doors while they go over him with a

88

Geiger counter. That may be just my uncontrollable imagination, but, anyway, this much is certain—the *Messenger* building is now a first-class security zone."

"And in words of one syllable?"

"Well, since early this morning no one's been allowed into the building without a signed pass, and throughout the day all telephone calls have been specially vetted and checked, but just what it's all about nobody knows. But I know. Or, at least, I know something. An inkling."

"But what's all that got to do with you being late?"

"I'm just coming to that," said Jim, sipping his sherry. "Well, I left the office at nine and went down to the Swan to have a rapid noggin with Archie and Joe. I'll admit that I over-stayed my leave a bit, but at twenty past nine conscience smote and I made a dash for the telephone to warn you I'd be a few minutes late. I dialled this number, but instead of getting it I found myself listening in on a crossed line. I heard: 'Hullo, Southampton? Ushercott here. . . .' and my ears pricked up of their own accord. After all, Ushercott isn't a common name, and I happened to know it as the name of the *Messenger's* circulation manager. Then I heard him say something to the effect that he'd be sending down double the usual batch, at which the Southampton man blew up something considerable. 'What's the idea?' he asked. 'Why, I can't shift what I normally get, and you know that. . . . What? . . . Special story, my foot! Why, I couldn't sell another copy in this district even if you'd scooped the Second Coming, and as for selling two copies where one sold before . . .' Words failed him, and then it was Ushercott's turn to become exasperated. 'Listen,' he said, 'and I'll give you a clue. It's Antigeos! And this time it's the real McCoy!' My heart went for a loop and then some oaf jerked open the door of the phone-box, bawled

'Sorry!' and cooked my goose. Ushercott heard the
interruption and warned the chap at Southampton that
there was someone on the line. 'I'll ring you back,' he
said. And that, as far as I was concerned, was that. Still,
it's quite something, isn't it? I mean, think of it—
Antigeos! And now all I want's an angle."

Deborah was merely looking bewildered. "It's no
good, Jim, I'm just not with you," she said. "I mean,
what is Antigeos? I thought it was a star or something."

Jim glanced at her wide-eyed before he remembered
how young she was, then he grinned and finished his
sherry. "Of course—twenty today," he murmured. "And
therefore only fourteen when the *Skylark* set off. So
let's eat and, while we're eating, I'll elucidate in all
directions."

They went up to the restaurant and Deborah, by
way of a birthday treat, settled for hot lobster and
a bottle of Liebfraumilch; and while they ate and
drank Jim expatiated upon Antigeos and the Pollenport
Expedition.

"I saw the take-off on a newsreel," he told her.
"Woomf, and the rocket took off! Wheee, and it was
gone! And then there was nothing but the commentator
saying, 'And so mankind steps out into limitless
space!'"

Deborah laughed. "Oh, Jim, you can't possibly remember what he said after five years!"

"Well," he said something like that, I'll swear it," Jim
told her. " 'Limitless space' came into it, and he
rounded off with: 'The *Skylark* forges on into the unknown, leaving the whole world to wait with bated
breath for the day when the intrepid Professor Pollenport and his companions will return to tell us what, if
anything, lies on the other side of the sun!' And now,
it seems, the world can unbate its breath, because

Sanderlake has the answer. Antigeos, as ever was, lies on the other side of the sun."

"But is it true?" asked Deborah.

"Well, if it's not, the *Daily Mess* is up to its neck in the biggest hoax ever perpetrated by a newspaper. On the telephone Ushercott said, 'It's Antigeos, and this time it's the real McCoy,' and then, when I came out of the box, I ran into two *Daily Mess* reporters, friends of mine both. Yes, Martin Way and Chip Carter, and they asked me to have a drink, whereupon, with my thoughts racing at twice the speed of light, I decided to try shock tactics. 'Thanks,' I said. 'Yes, let's drink to Antigeos and the joys of interplanetary flight!'

"Deborah, my sweet, that shook them. Martin looked at Chip, and Chip looked at Martin, and I don't think it would be putting it too high if I said that the blood drained from their faces. I said, 'So it's true, then?' and Martin hastily bought me a drink."

"And you got them to talk?" asked Deborah.

Jim nodded. "It was hard sledding, but, yes, I got them to talk. You see, Chip and Martin weren't the only *Daily Mess* boys in the bar and they were patently terrified lest I should breathe the word 'Antigeos' loud enough to be overheard, so I played that angle for all it was worth and in the end we struck a bargain. They undertook to tell me all they knew in return for my promise not to approach our news-editor with the story before morning. Of course, since they're not on the editorial staff they didn't know everything, but even so it seems that Antigeos is a fact all right and that Sanderlake has been getting radio signals from Pollenport ever since November——"

"November!" exclaimed Deborah. "Then why on earth hasn't he released the news before?"

"Because, he says, he wanted to be a hundred per cent

certain that he wasn't being made the victim of a hoax. Actually, it's more likely that he wanted to get all the facts into his hands before he gave any other newspaper the chance of horning in. . . .Well, now you've heard one part of the story, but the rest of it is even more sensational."

"Tell me."

Jim glanced round the restaurant and lowered his voice. "It seems that the Antigeosians are going to invade us," he whispered. "The Antigean army is on its way here in spaceships, and the *Daily Messenger* advises immediate mobilisation!"

Deborah went pale and nearly dropped her wine-glass. "War?" she breathed. "Oh, God . . ."

"Well, that's what Chip and Martin say, and don't ask me the answers to all the other questions, because I don't know them. I don't know how it was that Sanderlake, and no one else, got hold of the story. Or why Pollenport's allowed to transmit information about the invaders' plans. Or when we can expect the invasion. All I know is that this is the biggest band-wagon that's ever careered down Fleet Street, and somehow or other I intend to climb on to it. Now, dearest heart, can't you give me an angle?"

Deborah gazed at him across the table and frowned. "I don't know quite what you want," she told him. "Or what you mean."

"The point is I feel that I'm a jump ahead, yet can't think how to make use of it. My hands are tied until tomorrow morning, and by then everyone will have the news. . . . But, my God, there must be some way in which I can use the next nine or ten hours so as to keep a jump ahead!"

Deborah did her best to be helpful, but suggestions were hard to come by, and although the two of them lingered on in the restaurant, drinking coffee and smoking cigarettes, until everyone else had gone, their session was singularly unproductive. Their waiter hovered and hovered, and at last had to remonstrate mildly. "I don't want to hurry you, sir," he told Jim, "but we have to close in five minutes," and Jim looked at his watch to realise that it was just that many minutes short of midnight. . . .

It was snowing harder than ever as they left Bellamina's and the pavements were slippery with a coating of lumpy brown slush. Deborah started to cross the road towards the Haymarket, thinking to catch her bus, but Jim held her back. "I've got the car," he said. "I'll drive you home, but first we might as well have a coffee at the Mocha."

His arm was under hers, and she pressed it. "You shouldn't have brought the car out tonight," she said. "The roads are like skating rinks. Where is it?"

"Denman Street."

A blizzard was blowing across the Circus, and Deborah shivered and snuggled her face deeper into her fur collar. "They might put some clothes on Eros," she muttered. "He makes me feel even colder than I actually am."

Jim was gazing towards one of the Tube exits, where a small crowd was gathering. "What's going on?" he asked.

"A fight?" Deborah suggested, then caught a glimpse of a harassed newsvendor in a balaclava helmet. "Oh, no, they're only buying newspapers. The morning papers are out."

"The *Messenger!*" cried Jim, and hurriedly urged Deborah towards the Pavilion's marquee. "Wait there, darling, I shan't be two ticks."

The news was spreading like wild-fire, and the crowd

93   G

around the newsvendor was eight or nine deep. Jim squeezed his way into it and dragged twopence from his pocket as he went. At his side a woman asked of no one in particular what all the excitement was about and another woman answered her: "Dunno exactly, dear, but they say another planet's going to collide with the Earth or something. It's only in the *Messenger.*"

The newsvendor was a small man with a throaty voice several sizes too big for him. "'Ave yer tuppences ready!" he bawled. "Can't give change! Read all abaht it! Half a million monsters from Mars wiv frog-feet and dirty noses! Have yer tuppences ready!"

Then suddenly he waved aside the outstretched hands and shouted: "Last one left! Who'll give me what for it?"

"A tanner!" yelled somebody.

"Shilling!" from somewhere else.

"Two shillings!"

"Half a crack!"

"Five shillings!" bid Jim, and for a moment there was an awed silence until a sour-faced man with the look of a bookmaker's clerk shoved himself forward.

"Free half-crahns!" he grunted, holding them out.

"Ten shillings," yelled Jim, and that closed the bidding.

"Sold to the gent with the folding money," wheezed the newsvendor, and handed over the newspaper in exchange for Jim's ten-shilling note.

The crowd broke up and Jim made his way back to Deborah. "I got one," he told her, triumphantly, "but it cost me a half-slip. Now let's have a coffee at the Mocha and read all about it."

The Mocha was in Denman Street and they hurried in that direction through the driving snow. As they waited to cross Shaftesbury Avenue Jim took a quick

look at the *Messenger's* main headline. ANTIGEOS
DECLARES WAR! it said, and an icy tremor ran
through Jim's body.

Only express coffee was served at the Mocha, so that
was what they had to have and they drank it perched
on fixed stools as far away from the juke-box as they
could get. Jim spread the ten-shilling newspaper on
the counter between them and they weren't the only
ones to read it. At least half a dozen of the Mocha's
customers read it over their shoulders and their com-
ments made concentration difficult.

A quarter of the front page was given over to a sup-
posititious map of Antigeos on Mercator's projection and
compiled on the basis of Pollenport's descriptions of the
planet. And there were photographs—of Pollenport, of
Rose, of the *Skylark's* take-off and of Digby Cox.

Jim was so startled to see this last photograph that he
all but upset his coffee. "Digby Cox!" he exclaimed.
"Good God, I was at school with him. But what on
earth has he got to do with Antigeos?"

"He's the chap who picked up Pollenport's signal,"
said Deborah, studying another part of the page. "He
and his brother."

She pointed to a side-column headed: *The First
Signal—by Digby Cox,* and Jim fastened on it and read
the first paragraph.

"At Brydd?" he muttered. "But that's only about
eighty miles away! Let's go. . . ."

He gulped his coffee down and was deaf to Deborah's
protests. He folded the paper, stuffed it into his pocket
and slipped from his stool.

"But, Jim, it's after midnight!" said Deborah.

"That's right, and I can drop you on the way," he
told her, with shining eyes. "Unless you'd like to come
too?"

"I think you're mad. You know that, don't you?"

He laughed and swung open the plate-glass door. Snow swirled into their faces and Deborah hastily pulled up her collar. "Eighty miles in this!" she exclaimed. "Of course you're mad"

"But, sweetheart, this is just the angle I was looking for. This is the point where cub becomes ace. Why, for two terms, Cox major and I shared a study."

He took her arm and they ran across the street to the car. It was mantled in snow, and as Deborah climbed into the passenger seat Jim dragged a rug out of the back and tucked it round her. "Thank God I brought the car out," he muttered. "I damn' nearly didn't."

"You may have shared a study with Digby Cox," said Deborah, as the car slithered forward, "but that isn't to say he'll thank you for dragging him out of bed at about four o'clock in the morning. In fact, my guess is that he'll hate you."

Jim chuckled. "My sweet, I'm a newspaperman," he reminded her, "and when a rhinoceros wants to describe another rhinoceros as being thick-skinned he says, 'He's got a hide like a newspaperman!' In any case, the chances are that one of the Coxes will be on the job, transmitting and receiving. I don't suppose spaceships keep union hours."

He swung the car out of Shaftesbury Avenue into Coventry Street. "First Brixton, then Brydd," he murmured, under his breath.

"No, not Brixton," said Deborah. "I'm coming with you. All the way."

Jim gave an exultant whoop. "Now there's a girl with hair on her chest!" he exclaimed. "Deborah, the *Daily Post* is proud of you!"

Deborah laughed, but she was glad the next day was Saturday and that it was not her turn at the office. . . .

The jangling of a bell crashed through Bryan Cox's dreams and after a few seconds of it he put a hand out of bed and fumbled round for the alarm-clock.

The ringing stopped before he touched the clock and, puzzled, he opened his eyes. The clock's luminous hands said ten to four, and then he knew that the alarm couldn't have gone off.

"Extraordinary thing," he mumbled. "Must have dreamt it. . . ."

He heaved himself over on to his other side, pulled the bedclothes up closer round his ears and prepared to go back to sleep.

The bell rang again and he jerked himself up crossly, aware at last that it was the door-bell. He switched on the light and got out of bed, shivering.

He wrapped the eiderdown round his shoulders and padded across to the window. A full moon shining on the snow made the Square almost as bright as day, and the first thing Bryan noticed was an old-fashioned long-bodied car drawn up outside the shop. Then, as he threw open the window, two people stepped back into his line of vision—a man and a girl. The girl was so wrapped up that he could only see her eyes, but the man, tall and angular, he recognised at once as an ancient enemy.

It was Whacker Dawson, who had once given him six of the best for ragging in prep, and Bryan's bottom tingled faintly at the recollection.

Whacker grinned up at him. "Cox minor, isn't it?" he said. "Sorry to call at this ungodly hour, but——"

"I'll let you in," grunted Bryan, and slammed the window shut.

He put on his dressing-gown and slippers, and he was too dazed with sleep to wonder why Whacker Dawson should suddenly turn up at Brydd at four o'clock in the morning. He merely felt vaguely disgruntled, and as for being dragged out of bed, well, it was the sort of thing one would expect from Whacker Dawson. He never had had any respect for other people's feelings.

He ran down the stairs two at a time—not because he was anxious to let Dawson in, but because it was cold—and barked his shins against an electric ironing-machine as he crossed the shop. "For God's sake, come in," he muttered between chattering teeth as he dragged open the door. "It's as cold as the fifth circle of hell!"

Deborah took her head from her collar as she came in and now that Bryan could see her features he had to admit that Whacker Dawson had good taste.

"You must think we're dreadful!" she murmured, and Bryan grinned at her and decided that her voice was as attractive as the rest of her. In fact, he was inclined to think that she was far too nice for Whacker Dawson, who was now preventing him closing the door by stamping his feet in the doorway.

"Sorry, and all that," he was saying. "I mean, for hauling you out of bed, but the fact is that I've got to have the low-down on the Antigeos business. It's practically a matter of life or death."

Bryan at last managed to get the door closed. "Well, you'd better talk to Digby about that," he said. "He's on duty in the workshop. This way."

They followed him through the house to the back door. It was glazed and he pointed through the glass to the hut at the end of the garden. "That's where you'll find him," he said, as he opened the door. "You must excuse me coming with you, but I've only got slippers on."

"Not a remarkably warm welcome," whispered Deborah, as she and Jim picked their way along the snow-covered path.

"No, but we're in. And anyway I think we'll find Digby more affable. We were prefects together, which is to say I never gave him a beating."

"And Bryan you did?"

"Yes, I think I recollect something of the sort."

They arrived at the door of the hut and Jim knocked on it. He was answered by a muffled "Come in," and they went into the hut to find that Digby Cox believed in warmth and plenty of it. He had four electric fires burning, as well as three paraffin stoves, and the temperature would hardly have disgraced a Turkish bath. Digby himself was sitting in an armchair, reading, with a rug over his knees and an electric fire on either side of him.

He glanced round as Jim and Deborah entered and at once jumped to his feet. "Good God!" he exclaimed. "The Sensation of the Sixth! Jim Dawson, by all that's remarkable!"

He grasped Jim's hand and shook it. "Only I can't really believe it. People don't call upon people at four o'clock in the morning."

Jim grinned, and introduced Deborah. "We've just come down from London by car," he said.

"By car? God, you must be frozen solid, but I'm afraid I've nothing more exciting to offer you than beer. Or would you rather have tea?"

"Tea would be wonderful," said Deborah and, as Digby filled the electric kettle and plugged it in, Jim glanced cursorily over the radio equipment with which the hut was filled. The transmitter was easy to recognise, and so was the receiving set. He noticed that the latter was live. A small tell-tale was burning on its panel, but there was nothing emanating from the amplifier except the faint crackle of atmospherics.

Digby rejoined them and insisted on Deborah having the armchair. "Is this purely a social call?" he asked, as they settled themselves. "Or are there ulterior motives?"

Jim laughed. "I'm afraid there are," he said. "Actually, I've come to you to get the dope on Antigeos."

Digby glanced at him sharply. "Is the news out?"

Jim nodded. "Yes, in this morning's *Messenger*. I picked up an overnight copy."

Digby gave a short laugh. "Trust old Sanderlake never to tell me anything," he said. "I knew it would be soon, because they made me knock out an article for them earlier in the week, but I didn't think it would be as soon as this. So now the world knows?"

"Or will do in a few hours' time," said Jim; "and that's what I've come to see you about. It's the *Messenger's* scoop and I have the misfortune to work for the *Post*——"

"What, a reporter?"

"I'm afraid so, and now I'm hoping that you'll be able to give me something. Just a few crumbs such as might drop from Sanderlake's table."

Digby scratched an ear and was silent for some moments. "Well, it's difficult," he said, at length. "In a sense, I'm a *Messenger* employee myself, and therefore ethics and all that enter into it."

"I see," murmured Jim. "Then I'm sorry I spoke, but I'd got it into my head that you picked up Pollenport's original signals quite independently of Sanderlake, and then I took it that you simply sold him the story. I didn't realise that you were on the staff, as it were."

"Well, I am, and so's Bryan, and strictly speaking most of this equipment belongs to Sanderlake. Bryan and I were up to our eyes in debt when we picked up Pollenport's signal, so we went to Sanderlake with the news of it and he not only got us out of debt and helped us get new apparatus, but offered us a two-thousand-pound bonus if we could establish two-way communication with Pollenport within the month. Well, we made it, and then he said we could go on working for him if we liked, and he offered us a generous salary and a six-months contract. And we accepted."

"You do the whole job yourselves, do you?"

Digby shook his head. "No, we've a couple of chaps from the *Messenger* with us, and they live at the Red Lion. You may know them—George Bush and Phil Tarrant."

The kettle came to the boil and he got up. "Well, there it is, James," he said. "I'd like to help you, but my hands are tied."

He went to the other end of the hut to make tea and Deborah's eyes met Jim's. Her expression was a shade unfriendly and he could guess what she was thinking— that he'd made a fool of himself and of her. Success would have justified his impetuous eighty-mile drive through a freezing snow-storm, but nothing else could. and he reflected that he could hardly blame Deborah for feeling somewhat annoyed.

Her displeasure spurred him on to further effort, and getting up he tugged the *Daily Messenger* from his pocket.

"Well, is there anything you'd care to tell me off the record?" he asked, as he joined Digby by the tea-making bench. "I mean, if it's really a matter of war, I'd like to know just what we're up against."

Digby swung round. "War? What the deuce do you mean?"

Jim handed him the newspaper and when Digby saw the headline his eyes nearly popped out of his head. "Holy catfish!" he exclaimed. "Sanderlake must have gone nuts."

"I'll make the tea while you read it," said Jim. "I suspected that there might be a few inaccuracies."

Digby, scanning the lead-story, was as near to apoplexy as an innately placid man can get. "Inaccuracies!" he spluttered. "But this stuff's just lies from beginning to end."

"Sugar?" asked Jim.

Digby didn't hear him. "What's all this poppycock about an Antigean armada?" he snorted. "The armada consists of exactly one spaceship and, to the best of my knowledge, it doesn't carry a single weapon of any sort. Why, for the last week, Pollenport has been stressing that the visit is a purely friendly one, but there's not a word about that here. . . . And, oh God, what's this? 'All the evidence goes to suggest that for some time past Professor Pollenport and his companions have been prisoners of the Antigeosians, with the consequence that they have only been permitted to transmit messages at the dictation of their captors.' Now where on earth did Sanderlake get that idea from?"

"Do you take sugar?" asked Jim, patiently.

"Please. And milk."

Jim finished pouring out the cups of tea and carried the tray along to where Deborah sat. She was looking happier now, and as he handed her her tea she winked at him. "You've made an impression," she whispered.

Digby joined them without taking his eyes from the paper for a second. "But the whole thing's screwy," he protested. "Listen to this: 'According to Professor

Pollenport, the Antigean ruling class has almost nothing to recommend it and indeed its members, in their habits and outlook, are very little above the level of brutes. The Professor describes them as being pure albinos much given to feasting, fighting amongst themselves and maltreating their slaves and concubines. The slaves are kept in a state of subjection unknown on this planet at any stage of its history, yet hand in hand with this bestial slave-economy go technological achievements considerably in advance of our own. . . .' "

Digby broke off and glanced at Jim with an expression of exasperated disgust.

"Nonsense?" asked Jim.

"It is and it isn't," Digby told him. "The point is that there are two continents on Antigeos, a northern and a southern. The people inhabiting the northern continent are a decent lot, more advanced than we are in all sorts of ways, and they're the ones who are sending an expedition to visit us. But Sanderlake seems to have got it all balled up, and the description I've just read out refers only to a small race of creatures living on the southern continent. They could no more build a spaceship than a tribe of monkeys could, and anyway they're now almost extinct." Digby sighed and glanced at Jim. "What's your explanation?" he asked. "Sensationalism? Or sheer incompetence?"

Jim considered the question for almost a minute before he said: "Neither. If you ask me, Sanderlake *wants* to pick a quarrel with Antigeos. He wants to represent this visit as an act of war, so that he can prepare public opinion for an invasion of the other planet. Never forget that old Sanderlake is an imperialist of the deepest dye, and if you equate that with Cecil Rhodes's remark, 'I'd annex the planets if I could!' I think you'll see what's afoot."

Digby's lips tightened and for some moments he stared into space. Then he stood up abruptly and reached for two box-files from a shelf above the transmitter. He lifted them down and passed them to Jim.

"Jim, I'll give you a free hand," he said. "In one of those files you'll find a copy of every message I've sent Pollenport and in the other you'll find the text of every one of Pollenport's bulletins. I suggest you study them and then knock out an article giving the facts."

Jim was ecstatic and he made no attempt to conceal his ecstasy. "Digby, you're my friend for life," he cried. "From now on I'm a made man, and this is Success with a capital S. Tell me, am I to quote you, or how do we deal with that point?"

"No, for the time being, don't quote me by name," said Digby. "Just say you got your information from an unimpeachable source, and we'll leave old Sanderlake to draw what conclusions he likes." He waved towards a table on which stood a typewriter. "You can work there and I've got my own fish to fry."

"Meaning?"

Digby grinned and flourished the *Daily Messenger*. "I'm going to transmit the whole of this gobbledegook to Pollenport," he said, "and then he and the Antigeosians can act as they think best. And if they all decide to go back to Antigeos, it will just serve old Sanderlake right!"

He sat down at the transmitter and added: "The only snag is that I may not get through. Ever since the spaceship took off we've been picking him up all right, but he's only been getting us in fits and starts."

He switched on the transmitter, and Deborah offered to help Jim. They took the box-files over to the typewriting table and settled down to study the mass of typescript, making notes as they went along.

Digby sat and monotonously tapped out his call-sign, and when this had gone on for a quarter of an hour without evoking any response from the amplifier Jim glanced up. "Not getting you?" he asked.

"Can't tell yet. It takes ten minutes for my signal to reach them, and another ten for theirs to come back, making twenty in all."

"Good God, I thought radio-signals travelled as fast as light!"

Digby laughed. "They do, and that's the point. You know, the sun's light takes eight minutes to get to us, and the spaceship is a bit further away than the sun."

He had hardly finished speaking when the crackling of the amplifier grew louder, presently to resolve itself into the stutter of morse. "Yippee!" he exclaimed as he took up his pencil and pad. "That's it all right."

He listened for a few seconds, then tapped out a reply.

"That was Timothy Penn," he told Jim. "I've asked him to fetch Pollenport, which means we've another ten minutes to wait."

Deborah's gaze travelled to the window, against which the snowflakes were drifting. "I just can't take it in," she whispered. "I can't really believe that somewhere out there there's a spaceship and that it's signalling to us!"

"Well, if you can't, you can't," said Jim; "so let's get on with some work."

Nine minutes later the amplifier suddenly stuttered into life once more and Digby jerked upright. "Pollenport," he muttered. "So here goes!"

He spread out the *Daily Messenger* on the panel in front of him and put his hand on the morse-key, and for the next hour there was hardly a sound in the room except the steady tapping of morse, to be joined presently by the clacking of the typewriter as Jim started work on his story. Deborah could no longer be of any assistance, so she curled herself up in the armchair and almost at once went to sleep.

It was growing light outside by the time Digby finished transmitting, and by then his hand was aching and his eyes were tired. He stood up, stretched, and sauntered over to Jim. "That's the lot," he said, "and now we've twenty minutes to wait for Pollenport's reply. How goes it with you?"

"Read it," said Jim, and gestured towards the little pile of typescript. "I've practically finished, too."

Digby picked up the typescript and read it quickly, making occasional grunts of approval.

"Excellent," he said, when he finished it. "Definitely the goods. What happens next?"

Jim wound the last sheet of the story out of the typewriter and stood up. "I shall phone it in to the night editor," he said, "and he'll almost certainly hand it over to the *Evening Post,* which means that it will be on the streets by midday. You know, quite seriously, this is going to make my name."

"Fine," said Digby. "And now I suppose you want a telephone. It's in the shop. Come on."

The morning's post arrived just as they got to the shop and, while Jim went to the telephone, Digby picked up the letters from the floor and glanced through them. "H'm, one from his lordship," he murmured. "Now let's see what's on his mind."

He opened it and read:

Dear Cox,

By the time you get this letter the news will be out. For reasons of policy, I must now ask you to observe the following instruction, which is that in future you will transmit nothing to Pollenport without my specific approval. Now that the news of Antigeos is common property, our competitors will naturally be searching the ether for the relevant wave-length and therefore it is important only to transmit those messages that have been scrutinised and approved at the highest level.

I am also writing to George Bush on this matter, and it is his responsibility to see to it that my instructions are implicitly obeyed.

With kind regards,
Yours,
Sanderlake.

"Too late, old cock," murmured Digby, and handed the letter to Jim, who was waiting for his call. Then he glanced at his watch and decided it was time he got back to the workshop.

Deborah was sleepily filling the kettle as he went in and, trying not to yawn, she smiled at him. "I've just woken up," she said, "and I thought a cup of tea would be nice. What's been happening?"

"Nothing much," said Digby. "I finished transmitting the *Messenger* material and now I'm waiting for Pollenport to come through."

"Will he be long?"

"No, I'm expecting him any minute now," said Digby, but his expectation was not to be fulfilled. He waited twenty minutes—thirty—forty—an hour, and still nothing issued from the amplifier except the mutter of atmospherics.

Then, grey with anxiety, he tapped out another message to Pollenport: "Am getting nothing from you. Please advise if you received my last message. If the message was interrupted, please advise at what point and I will repeat."

Jim came in and informed them that Bryan was up. "He asked me to tell you that he's got some porridge on," he said, "if anyone feels like breakfast."

"I feel like it," said Digby, "but I can't leave the transmitter until George Bush shows up. Pollenport hasn't come through yet and I'm worried. Naturally, I'm not keen for him to come through when Bush is on duty, but there's nothing I can do about that. In any case, Bryan and I ought to go up to London and tackle Sanderlake."

"You mean right away?" asked Deborah and, when Digby nodded, went on, "Oh, good. Then you'll be able to ride with us."

The door of the hut opened and George Bush came in. He was a short thick-set man with a scrubby moustache and small inquisitive eyes. "Christ, it's cold——" he began, then broke off when he saw Deborah and Jim.

Digby made introductions, and Bush nodded perfunctorily. Then something about Jim seemed to strike him and he looked at him more keenly. "We've met before, haven't we?" he asked.

"Possibly. But I don't think so."

"Seen you somewhere, anyway," said Bush, then turned to Digby. "Anything startling?"

"Nothing. Just the routine exchange of call-signs each hour, and no messages."

"No? Well, now you can toddle off and get a bit of shut-eye. Are your friends staying?"

Jim answered him. "No, we just looked in in passing," he said. "And now we're on our way back to London."

"You know, it's funny, but I'll swear I've seen you before. Do you ever get down Fleet Street way?"

"I've been known to," said Jim, and then Deborah put her oar in.

"Jim, I'm sorry to interrupt," she said, "but we really must be getting along."

"Yes, of course," said Jim, and the three of them said good-bye to George Bush and left the hut. . . .

III

In London, and indeed throughout England, the feeling of tension mounted and in Downing Street a large and rather silent crowd collected outside No. 10. The weather was even colder than the day before, and all morning a fine powdery snow drifted down from low slate-coloured clouds.

Shortly after ten the police cleared a way through the crowd and a Rolls-Royce drove up and stopped outside the Prime Minister's house.

"Sanderlake," muttered the crowd, and as the newspaper-proprietor stepped out of the car he was greeted by a thin, tentative cheer. He acknowledged the cheer with a wave of his hand and a confident grin, then disappeared from view through the portals of No. 10.

"Dunno what they'd do wivout him," observed a small man with watery eyes and a scarlet nose. "They had to send for him to tell 'em what's what."

"I wonder they don't put the barrage balloons up, like in the last war," said a middle-aged woman at his side. "I was only a kid then, but I remember them all right. I come down here that Sunday with Mum and Dad, and all the balloons were shining like silver in the sunlight."

"Balloons wouldn't be no good against spaceships,"

said her companion, sniffing. "You have to have atomic weapons for them."

The crowd grew steadily larger, but for more than an hour nothing further happened. Then, at twenty-past eleven, the door of No. 10 opened again and Lord Sanderlake emerged. His expression was serious and he had the presence of mind not to wince or blink when sasha-lights flashed, splintering the winter gloom. Agency reporters crowded round him and asked him for a statement, but he shook his head and smiled blandly. "No comment as yet," he told them. "Later, we'll see."

"Will the P.M. be calling a Cabinet meeting?"

"I wouldn't know," said Lord Sanderlake, getting into his car. "Ask him!"

The crowd fell back as the big car moved off and Lord Sanderlake settled himself comfortably against the cushions and lit a cigar. He was well content with his morning's work. The interview with the Prime Minister had been all that he could have desired, and he would be a very surprised man if later that day he were not offered a place in the Cabinet.

The Rolls-Royce glided up Whitehall and into Trafalgar Square. Snow scudded like sea-spray across the façade of the National Gallery and on St. Martin's steps children were snowballing each other. Lord Sanderlake watched them with benevolent amusement and then, as the car pulled up for the lights, he saw something that startled him and caused him a sudden pang of uneasiness—an *Evening Post* contents bill. It said: ANTIGEOS—THE FACTS, and Lord Sanderlake hastily leant forward and spoke to his chauffeur.

"Breen, we'll have an *Evening Post*."

"Very good, m'lord."

The chauffeur pulled some coins from his pocket and

beckoned to the newsvendor, who shuffled out to the car. Lord Sanderlake practically snatched the newspaper from him and shook it open. He read:

ANTIGEOS: NO CAUSE FOR ALARM
Only One Spaceship on Way
'A Friendly Visit'—Pollenport

The *Evening Post* is proud to be in a position to state authoritatively

That all reports of an impending invasion by hostile Antigean forces are completely without foundation.

That the 'Antigean armada' referred to in some quarters consists of precisely one unarmed spaceship.

That this single spaceship is manned by fewer than thirty Antigeosians.

That Professor Jonah Pollenport and his companions are free agents and not, as has been suggested, the prisoners of the Antigeosians.

This information, and a great deal more, comes to us from an unimpeachable source and all of it based on messages transmitted by Professor Pollenport during the last few weeks. . . .

The car moved forward again and momentarily Lord Sanderlake took his eyes from the newspaper and glared angrily out at the snow. Then he resumed reading, chewing furiously at his cigar, and the more he read, the higher his anger mounted. His hands, holding the paper, trembled with fury and there was one thing of which he had no doubt at all—that whoever had written the story had had access, not only to all the material dispatched by Pollenport from Antigeos, but also to all the messages sent by the *Daily Messenger* to Pollen-port. It was possible, of course, that some unknown party had intercepted the transmissions, but he thought it unlikely. In fact, he suspected treachery, and, since only two complete copies of the material existed—his own and the one held by the Coxes—he told himself that he had not far to look.

The Rolls-Royce pulled up by a side entrance to the *Messenger* building, and Lord Sanderlake was out of it before it had properly stopped. He slipped on the frozen snow, nearly fell on his face, recovered himself, then hurtled through the doorway as if powered by jet-propulsion, and the force with which he threw himself into his private elevator all but jerked the cables off their pulleys. He slammed the gates shut and, as he rode upstairs, took one more glance at the *Evening Post* to keep his anger at boiling-point.

Dora Nutt, his principal secretary, was in his office when he erupted into it and as he struggled out of his overcoat he told her to get Digby Cox on the telephone.

Dora gazed at him coolly. "Mr. Cox is here," she told him. "He's waiting to see you. And his brother."

"What?"

For a moment Lord Sanderlake was caught off-balance and to conceal it he pulled out a handkerchief and blew his nose violently.

"Here, are they?" he snapped, when he had blown his nose enough. "All right. Show them in."

"Yes, Lord Sanderlake. And Mr. Keble-Keith tele-phoned. He would like to see you just as soon as it's convenient."

"Very well. Ask him to come round. I'll see him as soon as I've dealt with the Coxes."

As Dora left the office he dropped into his swivel chair, lowered his head so that his chin was resting on his chest and glared at the door through which the Coxes would presently enter. "Whippersnappers!" he told himself. "I give them their chance and at the first opportunity they sell me out!"

Digby entered the room ahead of Bryan, and Lord Sanderlake noticed that he looked tired and dishevelled.

"Sit down!" barked the newspaper proprietor, then glanced at Bryan. "And you."

Digby sat down, cleared his throat nervously, then squared his shoulders. "Well, Lord Sanderlake," he said, "so as not to beat about the bush, I may as well tell you that my brother and I have come out here to hand in our resignations."

A little taken aback, Lord Sanderlake frowned and thrust out his jaw. "Your resignations? Oh no, Mr. Cox—it's not as easy as that. For one thing, you're under contract, and for another——"

"Yes, we're under contract," agreed Digby, interrupting him, "and now we intend to break that contract. You can take us to court if you like, but I somehow don't think you will."

Lord Sanderlake simmered in silence for a few moments and reflected wrathfully that the interview was not going quite as he'd intended. He mashed out his cigar in the ash-tray, then immediately produced another and bit off its end.

"And may I ask why you intend to resign?"

Digby smiled wearily. "Of course you may. The fact is that we're disgusted by the way you're presenting the Antigeos story. All this talk about war. You must realise, Lord Sanderlake, that that's not at all in accordance with——"

Lord Sanderlake went purple. "What the hell's that got to do with you?" he roared. "You're on the reporting staff, not the editorial, and your job's to get the news and deliver it. And that's where it begins and ends."

"So it appears," said Digby, "and that's why we're resigning. We just don't care for being newspaper reporters. Of course, we realise we owe you something for the radio equipment and as soon as we've had time to get out the figures we'll send you a cheque."

Lord Sanderlake was hardly listening. He tugged the *Evening Post* out of his pocket and flung it on the desk. "And what about this?" he asked.

If he was hoping for a significant reaction from Digby he was disappointed. Digby merely glanced at the newspaper and shrugged. "Well, actually I haven't seen it," he said. "I'll have to get a copy."

Lord Sanderlake glowered. "What do you know about it?" he asked.

Digby glanced at his brother, then back again at Lord Sanderlake. "I've no comment to make," he said. "I'm sure you'll understand that with a possible legal action pending I must——"

"Legal action?" snorted Lord Sanderlake. "Yes, there'll be that all right—and more than one. I suppose you're aware, young man, that I hold exclusive rights in all Pollenport's material, and that now I'm in a position to take the *Post* people to court for hundreds of thousands of pounds?"

"No doubt you can, but I very much doubt if you will," said Digby, in even tones; "and, in fact, I'm rather sorry that's so. In my opinion, a good public airing of that sort would be very much in the national interest."

"The national interest?" choked Lord Sanderlake. "For thirty years I've been running the world's most widely sold newspaper, and you dare to talk to me about the national interest? I suppose you think you know more about that than I do?"

"Yes, I think so," said Digby, and for nearly a minute

he sat and looked Lord Sanderlake full in the face.

Then he glanced across at Bryan and said: "Come along, Bryan. Let's go!"

Lord Sanderlake was almost beside himself with frustrated fury. Impotently, he watched them get up and leave him, and when the door slammed behind them he could only sit and glare at it. Then it opened again and Bryan's head reappeared, and on his face was a disarming grin. "Good-bye!" he said, then slammed the door for the second time.

The newspaper magnate bellowed and leapt to his feet. "Irresponsible young fools!" he roared, and for some moments strode ferociously to and fro across the office. Finally, he fetched up against one of the glass walls and stood gazing glumly down into snow-shrouded Fleet Street. He blew cigar-smoke against the glass and, recoiling, it enveloped him in its greyish cloud. He coughed and spluttered, and at that moment Dora Nutt came in.

"Oh, excuse me, Lord Sanderlake, but are you all right?"

He choked and fumbled for his handkerchief to wipe the tears from his eyes. "Of course I'm all right," he gasped. "Why shouldn't I be? Can't a man cough without——"

He was interrupted by another paroxysm of coughing and Dora took the opportunity to straighten the things on his desk. "Mr. Keble-Keith is here," she told him. "Shall I show him in?"

Lord Sanderlake grunted and flung himself back into his chair. At that moment he felt that he'd rather not see Keble-Keith. If it hadn't been for that character he'd now have been sitting pretty. The news of Antigeos and all the rest of it would have been a tremendous story without any suggestion of invasion, and for that suggestion Keble-Keith was responsible. "I let him persuade me," muttered Lord Sanderlake, under his breath. "My God, I must have been mad!"

"I beg your pardon?" murmured Dora.

Her employer glanced up at her guiltily. "Nothing," he said. "Show Mr. Keble-Keith in."

Prosperity had not changed Keble-Keith. He still wore the same baggy unpressed brown suit that he had always worn, his hair still needed cutting and he had not troubled to replace his battered brief-case by a new one. There was, however, an unaccustomed glitter of excitement in his pale eye, and he was smiling.

"Congratulations, Lord Sanderlake," he said, flourishing a copy of the *Messenger*. "You've started things off with a bang!"

Lord Sanderlake glared at him balefully. "Seen the *Evening Post*?" he grunted, indicating the newspaper on his desk.

Keble-Keith laughed. "I've seen it," he said, dropping into a chair, "but I can't think that you're worried by it. What can the other papers do except either ridicule your story or ignore it? They haven't got any hard news."

"The *Evening Post* has. Young Cox has ratted on us, and I suspect him of giving the *Post* the free run of our files."

Keble-Keith clutched the arms of his chair and jerked himself upright. "What!" he cried.

"I've just this moment fired him," said Lord Sanderlake, and proceeded to give Keble-Keith a word-for-word account of the interview.

The financier lit a cigarette with trembling fingers and was silent for the best part of a minute. "We must stick to our guns," he said, in the end. "We must declare war on the *Post*! We must accuse them of play-

ing fast and loose with global security! We must——"
He broke off as a thought occurred to him, then asked:
"Has there been any Government reaction as yet?"

"Definitely," said Lord Sanderlake. "The P.M. had
me along there first thing this morning. I was with him
for more than an hour and now he's calling a Cabinet
meeting."

"You managed to convince him that the Antigean
intentions were hostile?"

"I think so. But at that time neither he nor I had
seen the *Evening Post*."

Keble-Keith snorted. "H'm, he can't pay any attention to that," he said. "The Government will have to
order mobilisation, or something like that. They'll be
too scared of dropping a clanger to do anything else."

Lord Sanderlake examined the ash on his cigar, then
looked up at the glass ceiling, which was darkened in
places by patches of snow. "It might be wiser to retract
a bit——" he began, but Keble-Keith interrupted him
by jumping up and towering over him.

"We can't!" he cried. "We're too deep in. We've
got to go on as we've started and, so far from retract-
ing, we've got to increase the pressure. Once those
Antigeosians land and start talking peace we're sunk
and you know it. We've got to rouse public opinion
into demanding militant action, and we've got to pull
everyone in on our side that we can. Otherwise, if anything goes wrong, you and I will be out on a limb and
we'll be made the goats. Yes, the owner of the *Daily
Messenger* and the managing director of the Anglo-
Antigean!" He stubbed out his half-smoked cigarette,
then asked: "No chance of buying Digby Cox off?"

"No. None."

"Where is he now, do you think?"

"I don't know. Probably on the way back to Brydd."

"And the equipment? What's the position on that?"

"The equipment?" echoed Lord Sanderlake, vaguely. "Oh, Cox said something about sending me a cheque in settlement, and no doubt he will."

Keble-Keith stared down at the newspaper-proprietor incredulously. "And you're letting him get away with that?" he asked. "You're actually letting him hang on to that transmitter, perhaps to put it at the disposal of the *Post*?"

Lord Sanderlake gnawed his thumb-nail and shrugged. "What else could I do?" he muttered. "Once he's paid for it, it's his. And in any case there's an old, but none the less true, saying to the effect that possession is nine points of the law."

"But, damn it, you've got a couple of your own men down there. That fellow Bush, he's a radio engineer, isn't he?"

"Yes, among other things, but——"

"My God, if you leave that transmitter there, you see what'll happen, don't you? Cox will tell Pollenport about the treatment you're giving the news-story and Pollenport will cut up rough. He'll probably advise the Antigeosians to go back to Antigeos, and then you'll be properly in the mulligatawny. You'll be made to look as if you've perpetrated the greatest newspaper hoax in history!"

Lord Sanderlake went white and started to sweat. Then he grabbed the nearest telephone and told the operator to get him George Bush at Brydd.

"It was a serious mistake," murmured Keble-Keith, as if talking to himself.

Lord Sanderlake glanced up sharply. "What was?"

"Why, letting those two young men get so much power into their own hands."

The newspaper magnate grunted, and any remark he

may have been about to make was interrupted by the telephone ringing.

"Bush?"

"Yes, Lord Sanderlake?"

"What's happening?"

Bush told him that nothing at all was happening. "I'm on duty," he said, "and there's been nothing from the spaceship all morning. I'm sending out a routine call-sign every hour, but I'm not getting any reply to it."

"I see. Well, now I want you to dismantle the transmitter, pack it on to a lorry and get it away from Brydd just as soon as you can. Take it to my place, Narraway Towers, and when you get there, telephone me."

"Very good, Lord Sanderlake."

"Try to get away before the Coxes return, but if you fail to and they complain, tell them to get in touch with me. Understand?"

"Yes, Lord Sanderlake. And what about the receiving set?"

Lord Sanderlake hesitated, then decided there was no need to put himself in the wrong unnecessarily. "No, not the receiving set," he said. "That belonged to the Coxes before we ever came on the scene. Just the transmitter. And get cracking!"

IV

When Digby told Lord Sanderlake that he and Bryan were tired of being newspapermen, he was not merely talking for effect, and later, in the dining-room of the Swan, he told Jim Dawson much the same thing. "Don't think we're not grateful to the *Post* for its offer," he said, "but the point is we want to be independent.

Having escaped from the *Messenger* we don't want to become embroiled with the *Post*."

"I suppose that's understandable," said Jim, "but where do we go from here? I mean, you can't just wash your hands of it all."

Digby agreed that they couldn't do that and then was silent for some minutes, while Jim eyed him anxiously. Jim had had a triumphant morning—he was now the *Post's* white-headed boy—and he had met Digby and Bryan at the Swan confident that they would help him consolidate his success. He had been sure that once they had broken with Sanderlake they would be prepared to transfer their allegiance, and he had told his news-editor as much. With the consequence that he was now considerably dismayed.

"I think it's possible that the *Post* would increase its offer," he remarked, when he could bear the silence no longer, "but I don't suppose that would make any difference?"

Digby shook his head. "None at all. No, the best suggestion I can make is that you come down to Brydd with us and take your chance. Obviously, we shall be keeping in touch with Pollenport and you ought to be able to pick up a story here and there."

Jim heaved a sigh of relief. "That will be fine," he said. "In fact, I could hardly have hoped for anything better."

"Then that's all right," said Digby, "as long as it's clearly understood that all the equipment is our property and that we shall use it as we see fit——"

Deborah came into the room and he broke off to draw out a chair for her. She had changed and, in spite of her sleepless night, she was looking fresh and cheerful. "Am I late?" she asked, as she sat down. "If so, I'm sorry, but I've had a wonderful bath and an hour's sleep, and now I feel ready for anything."

"A gin-and-French, for instance?" said Jim.

"Thank you. And what's been happening at this end?"

"Well, I've had my hour of triumph," Jim told her, "and, what is more important, the promise of a rise. Digby and Bryan have ditched old Sanderlake, and presently we're all going back to Brydd."

"Does that include me?"

Digby smiled. "Lovely to have you," he said, "if you can make it."

"Oh, I can make it all right. Tomorrow's Sunday."

The four of them had lunch at the Swan and spent most of the meal discussing the immediate future. "I suppose all the other papers will now start picking up Pollenport's messages," said Jim, "but there's no chance of any of them being able to build a transmitter in time, is there?"

"Good heavens, no," said Digby. "Why, the space-ship will be here in seven or eight days."

"So, in fact, the *Post's* sitting pretty? Of course, I realise that the transmitter's your property and all that, but you won't mind putting a few questions to Pollenport on the *Post's* behalf, will you?"

Digby grinned. "I dare say we can come to some arrangement," he murmured.

A big man with startlingly blue eyes in a startlingly red face came into the room and Jim nudged Digby. "That's Bernard Brayle," he murmured. "You've heard of him, haven't you? The *Post's* star reporter."

Digby nodded and glanced across the room.

The big man was about to sit down at a table when he caught sight of Jim and came over. He put a hand on Jim's shoulder, gripping it, and breathed whisky fumes over the four of them. "Congratulations, lad," he said, swaying a little. "Nice work, and there's room for it these days."

Then he lowered his head until his mouth was on a level with Jim's ear. "The Cabinet meeting broke up ten minutes ago," he whispered, huskily, "and it's mobilisation all right. Someone dropped the squeak, but we can't use it yet. The P.M.'s making a statement at three."

He nodded solemnly several times, then left them, and Deborah's eyes sought Jim's.

"Mobilisation?" she murmured. "That means that Sanderlake's getting his way, doesn't it?"

"Look's like it," agreed Jim. "Come on, let's drink up and get back to Brydd. For all we know, Pollenport's been trying to get us all morning." A thought struck him and he glanced at Digby. "Those two *Messenger* stooges, Bush and the other chap—I suppose they're still in possession?"

"I imagine so," said Digby, "but I can assure you that as soon as we get there they go out on their ears."

Jim grinned and stood up. "Come on. I can hardly wait."

They drove down to Brydd in Jim's car and during the course of the journey the thaw set in. The landscape became messily piebald and a thin khaki slush covered the roads. Beyond Bredinge Digby took note of a lorry coming towards them and recognised it for one that hailed from Brydd. "Old Bob Hancock is a long way from home," he remarked to Bryan, then suddenly, as the two vehicles passed, let out an exclamation and swung round to watch the lorry through the back window.

"What's wrong?" asked Bryan.

"Did you see who was sitting beside Bob Hancock?"

"No. Who?"

"It looked to me like George Bush."

Jim's eyes met Digby's in the driving mirror. "What do you infer from that?" he asked.

"I don't know," said Digby, "but I don't want to lose any time getting home."

The daylight was fading by the time they drove into Brydd, and as soon as the car pulled up, Digby jumped out and unlocked the front door. "Good Lord, it looks as if a young army has been tramping through here," he exclaimed, as he gazed at the muddy marks crossing the floor of the shop. "What the deuce has been going on?"

He hurried through the house and down the garden with Bryan at his heels. The workshop door stood ajar and he kicked it open.

"Christ, Bryan! They've taken the transmitter."

He strode into the hut and stared speechless at the place where the transmitter had been, and now there was no evidence of its tenancy except some marks on the wall and three unattached leads. Bryan noticed a letter propped up on the typewriter and handed it to Digby. "It's for you," he said. "From Bush, I suppose."

Digby ripped open the envelope and took out a sheet of flimsy on which a brief message had been carelessly typed:

Dear Cox,

Sorry about the transmitter, but we've taken it out on the Chief's instructions. He's the man to get in touch with if you've got any questions. Anyway, it belongs to him, doesn't it?

Yours,

G.B.

Jim and Deborah came into the hut as Digby crumpled the note and threw it into the waste-paper basket, and he pointed to the vacant space.

"It looks as if old Sanderlake had second thoughts after I left him," he said. "The transmitter's gone."

"God, he can't do that!" cried Jim. "It's larceny, pure and simple."

"Well, I suppose in a sense it was his," said Digby, "but when I told him I'd send him a cheque in settlement he didn't make any objection."

Bryan remarked that anyway they still had the receiving set and, as he spoke, he went across and switched it on. He turned up the volume and, after a few moments, the familiar murmur of atmospherics issued from the amplifier. "Just static," he muttered. "What the hell can have happened to Pollenport?"

"Let's have a cup of tea, and hold a council of war," said Digby, and went over to the sink to fill the kettle.

Most of the points brought forward during the council of war were negative ones. Clearly, since the spaceship would be arriving within a matter of days, it would be a waste of time to attempt to build another transmitter. Also it was obvious there was nothing they could do about Lord Sanderlake.

"We can't sue him," said Digby, "and we can't grab the transmitter back. In fact, we don't even know where it is."

"My guess is that it's at Narraway Towers," said Bryan. "We were within a mile or two of Bredinge when we saw the lorry, and if we want to make sure we can ask old Bob Hancock."

"Yes," agreed Digby, "but it doesn't help. Meanwhile, all we've got is the receiving set and we must keep it switched on day and night in the hope that Pollenport comes through. There are four of us, so we can cover the twenty-four hours with six-hour shifts and——"

"But you're the only one who knows morse," said Bryan, interrupting him.

"That's true, but whoever's on duty can blow a blast on a police-whistle and I'll come running."

As long as he lived, Digby would never forget the misery of that week-end. For one thing, it rained continuously, and with the rain came a warm enervating wind from the south-west. The four of them spent most of Sunday in the workshop, reading, playing a desultory game of poker, doing crossword puzzles and, at intervals, listening to the news bulletins. It seemed that the Sanderlake version of events was sweeping the world, and now not only Britain but half a dozen other countries, were preparing to mobilise. The spirit of confusion was abroad and with it went panic and a lot of loose talk about immediate atomic reprisals. The *Sunday Messenger* came out with a coloured supplement purporting to show daily life on Antigeos in a series of strip-cartoons, and on the radio eminent scientists, churchmen and politicians sought to outdo each other in wisdom and succeeded only in matching each other in fatuity. Everyone sounded very belligerent, but, as good luck would have it, the week-end's only casualty was a weather-balloon belonging to the Air Ministry. An anti-aircraft unit, manned by the Home Guard, fired on it and brought it down off Torquay.

Still no word came from Pollenport. . . .

Deborah, whose working week was spent as secretary to a shipper, caught an early train back to London on the Monday, and with her departure Jim became increasingly restless.

"I'm clearly not doing any good here," he said, "and I'm beginning to think I ought to get over to Salisbury Plain. It would be terrible if the spaceship arrived a few days early and caught me on the hop."

"I should give it another twenty-four hours," said Digby. "In any case, now that we've told Pollenport what's what, I imagine that the spaceship's landing plans have been revised."

Jim's gaze travelled to the amplifier. "Well, why the deuce doesn't Pollenport tell us something?" he muttered. "Still, I'll take your advice and stay another twenty-four hours."

And it was just as well that he did. . . .

Digby and Jim went to bed at about eleven that night, leaving Bryan on duty in the workshop. Digby didn't go to sleep right away, but, as was his habit, spent some time reading in bed. He was just thinking—at a quarter to twelve—that it was time he put out the light when he heard the police-whistle blow. He leapt out of bed, pulled on his slippers and struggled into an overcoat that he had put out for just such an emergency.

The whistle blew again, a long imploring blast, and he ran from the room and hammered on Jim's door. "Come on," he yelled. "Pollenport."

It was raining hard as he splashed across the garden, and in his hurry he lost a slipper and had to finish the journey with one foot bare. Bryan was waiting for him in the doorway of the hut and, in the background, he could hear the rattle of morse emanating from the amplifier.

"It's only just started," cried Bryan. "So far I think it's simply the call-sign."

Digby dashed past him and flung himself into the chair by the receiving set. He grabbed a pencil and pad, then relaxed a little. "Yes, it's only the call-signs," he muttered. "PL calling CX. . . . Thank God, he's come through again; I was getting seriously worried. Between you and me, I was beginning to suspect that the spaceship had been hit by a meteor, and destroyed."

The hut door opened again and Jim burst in, wearing a mackintosh over his pyjamas. "Why does news always have to break after the paper's gone to press?" he asked. "Is it Pollenport?"

"Yes, that's his call-sign."

Jim relieved Digby of the pad and pencil. "I'll take it down to your dictation," he said. "Then we'll all know what goes."

There came a pause in the morse and Digby touched the volume-control. "Here it comes," he murmured, and the words were hardly out of his mouth when the message started.

The morse crackled like machine-gun fire and Digby translated it in short bursts of words: "This is Pollenport on the Antigean spaceship calling Digby Cox at Brydd. . . . Have received nothing from you for more than forty-eight hours, but assume that the fault is with reception, as before. . . . I have serious news to impart and, in fact, this will be my last message. . . . Approximately sixty-seven hours ago a fatal accident befell the spaceship. . . . I was in the act of receiving a message from you and had just taken down the first sentence when the spaceship was shaken by a tremendous explosion and was thrown completely out of control. . . . Other explosions followed and later I learned that a combustion-chamber had burst, destroying a series of fuel-tanks. . . . My old friend and colleague, Sam Spencross, was killed outright, as were three Antigeosians, including our oldest friend on Antigeos, Quince. . . . Four other Antigeosians, one of whom has since died, were seriously injured and few of us escaped entirely unscathed. . . . Timothy Penn and I were flung from side to side of the radio-compartment and both the transmitter and the receiving set were badly damaged.

. . . For some hours all our attempts at repair were frustrated by the erratic movements of the spaceship as it somersaulted through space. . . . Later, the engineers managed to steady the ship by means of the undamaged motors, but we now have insufficient power to get under way once more. . . . Inevitably, we shall fall into the sun and already the heat is becoming almost insupportable. . . . It is, of course, impossible to say how many hours we have left to us before we lose consciousness, but, now that I shall not be returning to the Earth, I propose to fill in what time remains to me in transmitting information such as may be of service to future explorers. . . . During my sojourn on Antigeos I collected a great deal of scientific data to do with the planet's physical aspects and these are the details I now propose to give you. . . ."

There came a longish pause at this point and Jim caught Digby's eye. "Mind if I hand over to Bryan for a bit?" he whispered. "I want to go and telephone the office."

"Go ahead," said Digby, and as he spoke the morse was resumed, and this time it went on for hour after hour almost without pause. Digby grew hoarse with dictating and Bryan weary with writing, but Pollenport, a hundred million miles away, and facing certain death, seemed indefatigable. Relentlessly, he tapped out the contents of his notebooks for the last five years, and Bryan filled page after page of the pad with descriptions of the flora and fauna of Antigeos, and this was followed by masses of information concerning the planet's geological structure.

When Jim returned he took over from Bryan for a spell, but there was no one to relieve Digby and by the time the first streaks of daylight showed in the sky outside he was visibly flagging.

Then suddenly there came a break in the morse, and the three men exchanged glances.

"God, the end, do you think?" muttered Jim, and for five minutes they sat in silence visualising the horror of the spaceship's destruction.

Then, when they had given up all hope of a further message, the morse started up once more.

Digby translated: "Sorry . . . breakdown . . . terrific heat . . . apparatus affected . . . can't go on much longer . . . have been given euthanasia tablets, but doubt if I shall take mine . . . want to remain conscious for as long as possible . . . to be in at the death, as it were. . . . Prue has been given a tablet and is sleeping . . . Rose also . . . Timothy Penn and Paul Greenwood are with me . . . . another explosion . . . an Antigeosian comes in to tell me that fire has broken out in control-compartment . . . the fuel-tanks. . . ."

On that, abruptly, the message ended, and although Digby sat for several more minutes looking up at the amplifier he knew now beyond all shadow of doubt that the spaceship was no more.

Jim got up quietly and left the hut to telephone the news to his office, and Bryan pushed the pad and pencil from him.

"What a damned shame," he muttered. "To go through all they've been through and then to get half-way home and——"

He broke off and gazed glumly at the window's dim square of morning light. He was silent for some moments, then turned to his brother.

"I suppose there's no hope at all?"

"How can there be?" said Digby. "No, I'm afraid we've just heard the last lines of a tragedy and now the curtain's fallen."

Bryan got up and paced to and fro. "I don't imagine

we were the only people to pick up the message," he remarked.

"Unlikely. You can bet that since Saturday thousands of enthusiasts all over the world have been exploring the ultra-short wave-lengths. At least a few of them must have found the right one." He paused, then added, "I don't know, though. We must remember that it wasn't until a few hours ago that they had anything to tune to. Pollenport had been silent for more than sixty hours."

Bryan lit a cigarette and went over to the sink to fill the kettle. "Now I suppose old Sanderlake will start agitating for a fleet of spaceships to be built," he observed. "He'll never be happy until he gets the two planets fighting each other."

Digby laughed uneasily and said that it certainly looked like that. "Meanwhile, I bet the Army's feeling a bit silly," he said, "all dressed up and nowhere to go, now that the Government will have to scrap its fatuous scheme for mobilisation."

A few hours later they learned that they had not been the only ones to hear Pollenport's farewell broadcast. Sanderlake's organisation had picked it up, and the *Evening Messenger* came out with it almost simultaneously with the *Evening Post,* which meant that George Bush and his assistants must have worked like galley-slaves over the week-end to get an ultra-short-wave receiving set into operation in time.

As Digby predicted, the Government had to stage a quick climb-down, and that evening the Prime Minister once more spoke to the nation. After confirming newspaper reports of the spaceship's destruction, he pointed out there would now be no need for military preparations, and then he rounded off his statement with a graceful tribute to Professor Jonah Pollenport. . . .

CHAPTER VI

I

SIZE is a relative quality and, vast as the Antigean spaceship had seemed on land, in infinite space it was nothing. It was of less significance than an orange-box floating on an ocean, and impressions of the vessel's frailty had haunted Timothy Penn ever since the take-off; and now, when he first learned of Sanderlake's duplicity, these impressions gained in strength and threatened almost to overwhelm him.

He wanted to talk things over with Rose and, as soon as Pollenport could spare him, floated down from the radio-room to the living-compartment that he shared with the other humans. He was disconcerted to find no one there except Prue, who was in her bunk and asleep. He went out into the gangway again and was heading for the control-compartment when he came upon one of the engineers, a friendly young Antigeosian whose efforts to master English had so far met with little success.

"Have you seen Rose anywhere?" Timothy asked him, speaking slowly.

The Antigeosian smiled and gestured vaguely. "N'unnerstan'," he muttered.

"Rose. My wife. Have you seen her?"

"Ah, yes. I seen. He out. Out up."

"What, on the observation-gallery?"

The Antigeosian nodded vigorously. "Is where I seen."

Timothy thanked him and floated himself out on to the gallery, out of the benign artificial light of the gangway and into the sun's white and lifeless glare. For some time now, much of the sun's disc had been obscured from the spaceship by Mercury's dark mass and, since the spaceship was travelling faster than the planet, the part of the sun that was not eclipsed was gradually changing in shape. In fact, now the sun was only visible as a broad crescent of white fire, a crescent that would presently become a ring, until, later on, it became another crescent facing the opposite way. There was no other light on the gallery and when Timothy moved out of the glare he moved into darkness, an impenetrable darkness in which there was nothing to be seen except the star-clouds, but they were far clearer than we ever see them from the Earth and so beautiful that Timothy, in spite of the many times he had seen them before, caught his breath anew.

He came upon Rose almost at once, and she was alone, moving slowly round the gallery to keep the Earth in view. So far the Earth was no more than a brilliant point of light, indistinguishable from a bright star and only recognisable by its position, but Rose loved watching it. The others teased her about it, teased her about the amount of time she spent up on the gallery gazing at her home-planet, and day-dreaming.

Timothy touched her hand, making her jump. "What are you doing up here?" she asked, kissing him. "Aren't you supposed to be on duty in the radio-room?"

"Yes, but Jonah's taken over. That's what I've come to tell you about."

Rose sensed that something momentous was brewing, and her arm tightened about him. "What do you mean?"

"Digby Cox came through some time ago and asked

me to fetch Jonah because he had some important news for him. . . ."

The ship's rotation had brought them back into the sunlight and Rose's eyes searched Timothy's face. "What news? What are you being so mysterious about?"

"Nothing, except that it's not good news. Sanderlake has double-crossed us. He's telling the world that the Antigeosians are about to invade, that we're all prisoners and that—oh, a whole lot of nonsense."

Rose caught her breath. "But why?"

"Jonah thinks that he must have been got at by those interests that want to make trouble between the two planets. Stewart McQuoid's crowd. The boys who think that Antigeos would make a useful addition to the Empire."

"And?"

"Well, Jonah says we may have to go back to Antigeos."

Rose gasped. "No!" she exclaimed, and Timothy could see tears shining in her eyes. "No, darling, we can't go back!"

Timothy stroked her hand and pressed it. "Well, there's no point in trying to land on the Earth if we're going to be met with jet fighters and flak, is there?"

Darkness enveloped them again, and after a moment or so Rose asked him what her father had told Digby Cox.

"Nothing," said Timothy. "He simply hasn't replied to the message. He wants to consult the Antigeosians first and, you see, now that the news is out, all sorts of people may be picking up our transmissions."

"But we can trust the Coxes?"

"Oh, of course. Otherwise, they wouldn't have told us what was happening, and we'd have sailed slap into it. . . . God, what swine! Sanderlake and his crowd, I mean."

Rose put her cheek against Timothy's, hugging him. "Oh, Timothy, say we don't have to go back!" she whispered. "I'd sooner face anything than that. Fighters, flak, anything! All I can think about is home! . . ."

II

More than sixty hours passed before any decision was taken, and Rose found those hours the most terrible she had ever had to endure. For sixty hours everything was at a standstill, while Pollenport and the Antigeosians conferred, and all that time the giant spaceship simply wallowed in space, going neither forward nor backward, but exerting just sufficient power to counteract the gravitational pulls of Mercury and the sun.

The humans took it in turns to man the radio-compartment and Pollenport's instructions regarding it were unequivocal. No transmissions whatsoever were to be made to the Earth, and the activities of the person on duty were limited to keeping notes of all messages received. Regularly every hour the station at Brydd came through, giving its call-sign and imploring the spaceship to reply; and also, now that the whole world knew about Antigeos, a number of other signals were picked up. For the most part they came from amateurs who were painstakingly searching the ultra-short wavelengths in the hope of establishing contact, while there were a few that emanated from commercial interests that hoped to do a deal with Pollenport. In fact, during the course of those sixty hours, he was offered any number of vast sums to appear in films, on television

134

and on the variety stage, or to endorse products that ranged from soap-powder to indelible ink. And for Rose came the offer of three hundred thousand dollars to play the title-role in a film called *Spaceflight Floozie,* and she couldn't make up her mind whether to feel flattered or insulted.

It so happened that she was on duty in the radio-room when at last the decision was reached, and Paul Greenwood came to her grinning all over his face. He was the only one of them that Pollenport had taken into his confidence during the course of the discussions, and now he said: "Okay, Rose. I'll take over, because Jonah wants you all to assemble in the living-compartment. The verdict's been arrived at."

Rose jumped up and faced him. "Aren't you going to tell me what it is?" she asked, then suddenly realised the significance of his cheerfulness. "Oh, we're going on, aren't we, Paul? Aren't we?"

"Maybe. You go and hear what Jonah's got to say."

As Rose floated herself towards the door, the rumble of the motors suddenly swelled until it became a subdued roar, and she paused, steadying herself against the door-post. "Paul, they're opening the throttles!" she exclaimed. "We're moving again, thank God!"

She waved blithely and went down to the living-compartment, arriving there simultaneously with Pollenport and Quince. She noticed that her father looked tired and troubled, anxiety shadowed his face and he had not shaved for two or three days; and Quince, who had attended the discussions as interpreter, was also wearing an unusually serious expression.

Timothy and Sam had just finished a game of chess, and Rose joined Timothy and settled herself between him and Regan, who was helping Prue with a jigsaw puzzle. The puzzle had been specially designed for use on the spaceship, and each of its pieces had a tiny magnet embedded in it to keep it from floating away.

Rose asked Timothy if he'd heard the news.

"Not officially," he told her. "But I gather we're resuming the journey."

"I know. It's wonderful, isn't it?"

"Well, yes. But let's hear what Jonah's got to say."

Pollenport steadied himself against a stanchion and told them that a decision had been reached. "We're going to continue on our way," he said, "and land on the Earth, but before you all start cheering I'd like to say something about the difficulties involved. As you know, certain interests are doing all they can to stir up animosity against the Antigeosians. The spaceship's visit is being represented as an act of war, and already some Governments, including the British, have been panicked into something approaching mobilisation. Consequently, if we were to land without taking precautions it is almost certain that we should be fired upon. Therefore, our first step must be to persuade the people of the Earth that they stand in no danger from us. We can't hope to do that by radio since we shall merely be suspected of trickery, and so we've evolved a more elaborate plan. We're going to suggest that the spaceship has come to grief, that one of the motors has blown up and that the vessel itself is derelict and falling into the sun. Again, we may be suspected of trickery, but as regards that we can only take our chance and hope for the best. If, on the other hand, we manage to carry conviction, I think we can safely say that all plans for mobilisation will be dropped, with the result that we shall at least be able to land all in one piece. Naturally, the landing plans have had to be revised. Salisbury Plain is out of the question and instead it is proposed that we land the spaceship on Pengeness Marsh, touching down before daybreak and while it is still dark. The Coxes are the only people in England that we know we can trust, and that's the reason we've chosen Pengeness for the landing. A number of us—probably myself, Timothy, Rose, Prue, Regan and Quince—will disembark and then the spaceship will take off again. We of the landing party will walk into Brydd and make ourselves known to the Coxes while the spaceship hangs around in space awaiting our instructions. I shall take the Antigean credentials with me, of course, together with a small amount of gold to enable us to buy clothes and anything we may want in the first few days, and Sam and Paul will stay with the spaceship to work the radio. As soon as we manage to establish good relations with the Government we shall radio the fact to the spaceship and it will then make its official landing. Well, I suppose all that sounds delightfully simple, as is the habit with plans, but, of course, we must be prepared for all sorts of alarms and excursions. The Sanderlakes of our world are not given to surrendering anywhere short of the last ditch and so, while I hope we can avoid violence, we mustn't be surprised if it's offered us. I don't think there's anything more to be said except that I hope it keeps fine for us."

He was smiling faintly as he finished and the expression of the others was rapturous. Timothy was the first to speak and he asked a question more from the need to say something than because he couldn't guess the answer. "I suppose," he said, "the embargo on transmissions to the Earth still holds? I mean, between now and when we fake the disaster?"

"Yes, of course," said Pollenport. "I'm going to tell the Coxes that the radio was damaged when the motor exploded, which will explain our long silence. For our final transmission, I think it would be a good idea to work out something in the way of a script, and if any of you would care to give me a hand with it I should be grateful. I can't say that I'm enamoured of all this deception, but I'm afraid it's rather been forced upon us."

Prue was getting bored with all the talk, and now she claimed Rose's attention by catching hold of her hand. "I've nearly finished the jigsaw, Mummy," she said. "Yes, while Grandpa's been talking I've nearly finished it. I think it's easier if nobody helps me."

Rose laughed and told her daughter she was an ungrateful brat. "The first thing that happens when you get to England," she said, "is that you go to school."

"Where the animals go?" asked Prue, eagerly.

"No, you idiot child. That's the Zoo. School is where little girls go."

III

As the spaceship neared the Earth, the humans, together with Quince and Regan, inclined to spend all their time on the observation-gallery, and it was from there that they had the closest view of the Earth's moon ever granted to mankind. The spaceship passed within about seven hundred miles of it and at that distance the satellite was almost too vast to be accepted as a globe. It was more a great curving wall of silver light that blotted out one whole section of the heavens.

Pollenport, Sam and Paul got busy with cameras and photographed the moonscape continuously, concentrating particularly on those aspects of it never seen from the Earth. Through glasses, Rose surveyed the deserts and craters, and presently she discerned thin bluish clouds of vapour or dust streaming and swirling across the lunar surface.

"Daddy, I can see dust-storms or something like them!" she exclaimed. "But that's impossible, isn't it?"

Pollenport laughed and borrowed the glasses. "Well, it isn't if you can see them, is it?" he murmured, as he raised the binoculars and adjusted the focus.

"But I thought there was no atmosphere on the moon?"

"That's what we've been led to believe," said Pollenport, "but it's not entirely impossible that there should be one."

They could see the Earth plainly now, five times larger than the moon as seen from the Earth, and the familiar shapes of its oceans and land-masses tugged at Rose's heart. The southern half of Africa was easily recognisable and she lifted Prue up to see it. "And can you see an island to one side of it?" she asked. "That's Madagascar."

"Is that where you used to live when you were a little girl?"

"No, darling. . . ."

"But you told me you lived on the island. With Grandpa."

"Oh yes, but there are lots of islands on the Earth. Many more than there are on Antigeos, and the one we're going to, and where I lived, is called England, but we can't see it yet. As soon as we can see it, I'll let you know."

"All right."

During the next few hours the excitement was so pervading that Rose found it impossible to eat or sleep, and difficult to think or talk or do anything at all except watch the Earth as it slowly approached. When she had been thirty hours without sleep, Pollenport intervened. He told her to go and lie down, and made it an order. "Otherwise, when we land," he said, "we'll have to leave you behind on the ship, and I'm sure you'll hate that."

"Yes," said Rose, and obediently went to the sleeping-compartment. She lay down and, in fact, did manage to sleep for a while, but she was presently awakened by a change in the noise made by the motors.

She sat up quickly and gazed about her. She was alone, except for Prue who was asleep, and urged on by the fear that she might be missing something, she scrambled into her tunic and went up to the observation-gallery.

Timothy was there, with Quince and Regan, but there was no sign of the other humans and Timothy explained that they were in the control-compartment. "I think final preparations for the landing are being made," he said, "and anyway this is where we kick our heels for a bit."

"What do you mean?"

"Didn't you hear the motors throttle down? They've practically stopped them and for the next few hours we shall fall round the Earth until it's time for us to land."

Just then the ship's rotation brought the Earth into view and Rose was astonished by its nearness. "Look," she breathed, "Europe! . . . How far away are we, Timothy?"

"Only about a thousand miles."

As throughout the journey, the Earth had its sunlit side towards them, but they could see the fringe of night lying across Asia and within a few hours it would cover Europe. "And when dawn comes to England, we land?" murmured Rose.

"That's right. But by then we shall have been round the world five times! . . . We're not standing still, you know."

Rose put an arm round him and hugged him. "Oh,

think of it, darling! Within twelve hours we shall be breathing English air and treading English soil."

"Mud," suggested Timothy. "Pengeness is mainly mud. . . ."

Chapter VII

I

IT was still dark when Luggy Martin came out of his cottage and got on to his bicycle. He headed towards the Marsh, moving as silently as a ghost along the road that led out to the lighthouse. There was no lamp on the bicycle and it is doubtful if anyone except Luggy could have ridden along that road in the dark without coming to grief. He knew the Marsh as a dog might know it, by scent and by sound, and he knew it far better than did the warden whose job it was to protect and preserve the Marsh's wild birds from such as Luggy.

The morning was calm and cold and the absence of stars told Luggy that the sky was clouded. Twice every three minutes the beam of the lighthouse swept the Marsh and by its flash Luggy could see that a mist lay over the stretches of mud and water, a white mist so shallow that it would hardly come up to a man's knees.

"Just what the doctor ordered," muttered Luggy, and when he had ridden about a mile he stopped pedalling and dismounted. He lifted the bicycle to the side of the road and hid it in a patch of reeds. He waited for the next flash and then started forward, making for a stretch of water shaped like a boomerang over on his left. He was wearing Wellingtons and the turf underfoot was heavy and sodden, but an otter couldn't have made less noise than Luggy as he moved through the mist.

Now in the eastern sky there was a trace of light, pale

and smooth, and presently, when Luggy was about ten yards from the L-shaped pool, he dropped to his knees and crawled forward until he came to the rushes that grew at the water's edge. He thrust his hand into his waterproof jacket and pulled out a heavy air-pistol.

Slowly the light grew stronger and after a while Luggy wriggled steadily round the pool's edge until he came to a break in the rushes through which he could see the surface of the water with the mist lying on it like smoke. Several ducks were asleep on the pool, and the nearest was a drake so close that Luggy could almost reach out and touch it, and his predatory heart swelled a little. The drake's head was tucked under its wing and Luggy drew a bead on it, aiming just behind the eye.

Plup. . . !

The drake gave a single convulsive jerk as the slug hit, and its head shot out from under its wing, open-beaked. The rest of the birds took fright, rising from the surface almost as one, but breaking its surface into a dozen short, spreading wakes, and by then the dead drake had keeled over on to its back, with its webbed feet feebly beating the air.

Luggy got to his feet and, as his head came above the level of the mist, he automatically looked up at the wheeling duck—and it was as if he had stood up into a nightmare. The sky above him was blotted out by a vast black disc, a disc that hummed softly and seemed to be descending directly upon him.

He let out one fearful lunatic scream and then ran howling towards the road. His heart threshed as if it had broken loose and a frantic prayer raced through his mind: "O God—get me out of this and I'll never go poaching again!"

He stumbled and fell headlong into a mudpatch.

Instinctively he covered his head with his hands and for fully a minute he lay there sobbing and moaning, and too terrified even to try to get up. The noise the great disc was making grew louder until all the air seemed to throb with it, and at last Luggy plucked up enough courage to raise his head and look back over his shoulder.

Fifty yards away the spaceship was settling down on to the Marsh, settling as gently as thistledown and, almost beside himself with relief, Luggy scrambled up. The thumping of his heart quietened down and for a minute he stood there staring incredulously at the spaceship and asking himself what the blinking hell it could be.

Then he started towards his bicycle, moving crabwise so that he could keep his eyes on the enormous machine, and when he reached the bicycle he lay down among the reeds and waited, without taking his gaze from the spaceship for a moment. Against the sky's pallor he could just make out the air-screws of the helicopters gently turning and then on the machine's underside he glimpsed a lozenge of yellow light, as if a hatch had been opened. Dark figures moved against the light, and he guessed that some of the spaceship's crew were disembarking. For a moment vague terrors gripped him and he told himself that if he had any sense he'd jump on to his bike and ride like the devil, but, in the long run, his curiosity proved stronger than his fears. . . .

The spaceship's mass hid the lighthouse from him, and some time passed before he could make out quite what was happening. Then the air-screws started to revolve more quickly and the lozenge of light vanished again, as if the hatch had been closed. A faint patch of light still showed, however, and Luggy had the impression that one of the men who had disembarked was holding a torch.

The spaceship began to rise, lifting from the Marsh as easily as a gas-balloon, and presently the lighthouse's beam passed under it to pick out a small procession of figures moving towards the road. Luggy counted five of them and they advanced slowly, picking their way between the pools and the mudholes, and as they came nearer Luggy saw that the leading figure carried a stick with which he tested the ground ahead of him.

The spaceship was rising quickly now, so quickly that Luggy could almost see its dark mass dwindle as he watched, and the sky was growing lighter with every minute. Luggy reckoned that the little procession would reach the road at a point about twenty yards north of him—twenty yards nearer Brydd—and so there was no risk of his being seen. They were talking a little among themselves, but he could not make out what they were saying or, indeed, whether or not they were speaking English.

The leader was a big man with an impressive shock of grey hair and he was followed by a girl carrying a child, and, although the light was still too poor for Luggy to be able to make out their clothes in any detail he was aware that they were not dressed conventionally. "Foreigners, I shouldn't wonder," he told himself. "I reckon they have foreigners on other planets the same as we have."

They gained the road, then turned towards Brydd, walking quickly. Luggy raised himself cautiously, at which two of the five people turned and gazed in his direction exactly as if they heard him move. Yet Luggy was certain that he had not made a sound and he was puzzled. Meanwhile, he held himself absolutely still, almost to the point of holding his breath. The two strangers were still gazing in his direction, and now their leader also stopped, and glanced round.

"What's wrong?" he called, and he was answered by another man.

"Quince and Regan say that something moved behind us."

"Oh, an animal, I expect," said the leader. "A hare or a rabbit. I can't think that there'd be anybody out on the Marsh at this time of morning."

Luggy grinned and thought, 'That's all you know about it, cock. Only I must say your pals have got damned good earsight. No bird could have heard me, so I don't see how a person could.'

He waited until the strangers had gone another twenty yards along the road, then stooped to reclaim his bicycle. At once the two who had turned before glanced round, and Luggy stiffened. 'Beats me,' he reflected. 'Anyone'd think they were fitted with wireless or something.'

This time he waited until they were nearly a hundred yards away before he moved and when at last he picked up his bicycle he was relieved to see that there was no reaction from the strangers.

Luggy was not a man of wide experience or deep learning, but he had a brain that could put two and two together to his own advantage and, as he cycled very slowly along in the wake of the visitors, he reflected that if he boxed clever and handled this business right he ought to be able to make himself a quid or two. "I reckon they got something to do with them two Coxes," he told himself. "And, if so, we'll find out what Cousin Bob Hancock's got to say about it. . . ."

The grey light of a sunless dawn filled Brydd's streets by the time the strangers reached it and Luggy, anxious to see where they were making for, took the risk of narrowing the gap that separated him from them. When he was about forty yards behind them the same two as

146

before swung round, then pointed. Luggy had no choice but to ride on and, as he came abreast of the little group, their leader addressed him.

"Good morning," he said. "Can you please tell me where we'll find Mr. Digby Cox's radio shop?"

Luggy dismounted shakily, and swallowed two or three times before he was able to reply, and his mind was mainly occupied with what he'd have to tell the company in the Dolphin that evening: "All five of 'em, grown men and women, in sort of padded pinafores. Coloured 'uns, and didn't hardly come down to their knees. And then there was them two queer 'uns with things sticking out of their heads like snails' horns and their eyes as round as an old cat's. And there was me and my old bike actually talking to 'em and wondering if they mightn't be poisonous or something."

He wiped his mouth on the back of his hand and avoided Pollenport's gaze. "In the Square," he said, hoarsely. "That's where you'll find Mr. Cox. At the wireless shop in the Square. The end of this road and turn right. You can't miss it—it's in the Square."

Then before Pollenport could thank him he leapt on to his bicycle and rode off. He rode through the Square and didn't stop pedalling until he came to a cottage on the outskirts of Brydd. The cottage was flanked by a couple of petrol pumps and a large shed, and across the shed's double doors were painted the words: *R. Hancock. Haulage Contractor*.

Luggy leant his bicycle against the fence and went round to the back of the cottage. A light was burning in the cottage and through the window he caught a glimpse of Bob Hancock shaving at the sink.

Luggy rapped on the door. "Hey, Bob! It's me, Bob— Luggy."

He heard his ancient cousin shuffle across to the door

147

and then came the sound of bolts being drawn and the latch lifted. Bob Hancock had a towel in his hand and with it he was wiping the shaving-soap from his face. "Up betimes, aren't you?" he grunted.

"That's right, Cousin Bob," agreed Luggy. "Fact is, I've come to ask your advice."

Old Hancock grunted again and with a jerk of his head invited Luggy in. "Well, don't stand in the doorway there," he muttered. "I don't want to give welcome to all the cold air in Brydd."

He was a severe old man to look at and one who was never known to smile. He was thin and shrunken and his grey, drooping moustache emphasised the general air of gloom that hung about him.

"Haven't seen you in chapel of late," he observed, as he poured a little hot water into the tea-pot and swiggled it round. "I suppose you can get along without the Lord these days?"

Luggy ignored this. "Cousin Bob," he said, "something amazing's happened to me, and that's what I want your advice about. Yes, what'd you do if you'd been out on the Marsh this morning and had seen a blooming great spaceship come down?"

Bob Hancock gazed at him coldly, and sniffed. "First thing, I'd promise myself to keep out of the Dolphin at nights," he said, "and second thing, what were you doing out on the Marsh that early?"

"Well, I was sort of——"

"After duck, eh?" grunted the old man. "Well, you're a fool, Cousin Charles, and it'll only be a matter of time before the warden catches you. And apart from him, one day you'll have another Warden to reckon with, and One that sees all things even to the fall of a sparrow. And if a sparrow's not too humble for His notice, 'tisn't likely He'll ignore a duck!"

148

"That's right, Cousin Bob," said Luggy, "but I'll swear I wasn't out after no duck——"

"I suppose you want a cup of tea?" asked the old man, as he took a cup fom the dresser and slammed it down on the table beside the two that were already there.

"Thanks," said Luggy. "Yes, it'd come in handy."

He knew his Cousin Bob. You had to take things at his pace or you got nowhere at all, so Luggy said nothing more for the moment and watched the old man tremblingly pour out three cups of tea.

"How's Cousin Milly?" he asked, as the old man picked up one of the cups and moved towards the door with it.

"Suffering and sorrowing," said Hancock. "She'll get worse before she gets better, and then perhaps she won't get better at all."

He left the room, and Luggy supped his tea noisily. Old Bob was a crusty old devil, he reflected, but he wouldn't mind betting that he'd come round surprisingly as soon as he learned there was a bit of money concerned. "We ought to clear a hundred nicker each," he told himself, "and that's putting it low."

Presently Bob Hancock returned. "Now, what's all this gammon about a spaceship?" he asked.

"I'm telling you, Cousin Bob, and it wasn't no dream. It come down within a mile of my cottage and it was a blooming great thing near as wide across as Brydd Common. Five folk got out of it—and two of 'em wasn't human beings!"

"You mean it's still there?"

"No, it took off again, but the five what got out of it come into Brydd—and I spoke to 'em!" Luggy paused for effect, then added: "They asked the way to the wireless shop and I reckon that's where they are now. And

149

it strikes me that you and me might turn ourselves an honest penny or two."

Old Hancock's eyes narrowed. "I don't see it," he muttered. "Just what have you in mind, Cousin Charles?"

"Well, we know that Lord Sanderlake had a bit of a do with the Coxes, and you helped his chaps get their gear out and take it to Bredinge. And then the Coxes got hooked up with the *Daily Post,* and the next thing we heard was that the spaceship had come to grief. Now I reckon that that's where they tricked Lord Sanderlake. I reckon that the Coxes and that Professor and the *Daily Post* carved it up between them, and the *Daily Post* said to the Professor, 'Do you land nice and quiet out on the Marsh, and then we'll keep the news to ourselves till it suits us to give it out. . . . Well, that's what I reckon happened, and it strikes me that Lord Sanderlake'd pay a nice little bit of money to know what we know. To my way of thinking, he might even go up to five hundred quid."

Bob Hancock put his cup down and wiped his moustache. "If it isn't all a pack of lies," he said ungraciously. "If you think there's all that money in it, why did you come to me? Not out of family feeling, I'll be bound."

"Well, there is that," said Luggy, "but it was more on account of your lorry. With the lorry we could be there in an hour and a half, when it'd take me damnnigh four hours on my old bike. Besides, you've been there and they know you a bit. More chance they'll listen, like."

The old man poured himself out another cup of tea. "Well, I don't count on wasting my time and petrol for nothing, you know," he said. "Either I come in half-and-half, or not at all."

Luggy nodded. "Yes, that's all right," he said.

"Then I'll tell you what I'll do," said his cousin. "You and I will drive down to the Marsh in the lorry and, if we can see the marks where the spaceship landed, well and good. But if it turns out you've been stringing me a pack of lies, well, Cousin Charles, from now on I'll leave you out of my prayers and likewise my will!"

II

If Antigeos seemed a strange place to the humans on their first arrival, Regan's and Quince's first experience of the Earth was far stranger, and not nearly so pleasant. For one thing, there was the darkness and, for another, the cold. Quince followed Pollenport down the ladder from the spaceship and the first step he took on the Earth filled his shoe with water and liquid mud. Regan came next and she was followed by Rose, with Prue in her arms, and last of all came Timothy. Prue, worn out by excitement, was almost asleep, and, even when Rose whispered that they had arrived, she merely mumbled something and pressed her face closer into Rose's neck.

Pollenport, carrying a stick and a torch, told the others to follow him in single file and to keep as close to him as they could. "From what I remember about Pengeness," he said, "somewhere ahead of us there's a road that connects Brydd with the lighthouse."

The lighthouse—that was the first of the many mysteries that Regan was to encounter and as its beam swept the Marsh she asked Rose what it was, and Rose, remembering the Antigeosians' strange attitude to ships, hesitated to tell her. "I can't explain now," she whispered. "Some other time . . ."

Behind them the spaceship rose slowly into the air, and now that their eyes were growing accustomed to the semi-darkness they could gain some impression of their surroundings.

"Is all England like this?" asked Quince, as he surveyed the waste of sodden turf and water."

Timothy laughed. "Good heavens, no. The scenery changes every few miles. You'll see."

They gained the road and a few moments later Quince and Regan sensed a movement behind them by means of their antennæ.

"Someone moves" whispered Quince. "Behind us."

Pollenport told them that it was probably a small animal, but Regan knew that he was mistaken. She was sure that the movement had been made by something at least as big as a human being, and her hand sought Quince's.

Pollenport said: "To the best of my recollection, Brydd's about a mile and a half ahead, so it should be almost full daylight by the time we get there."

"A mile and a half?" murmured Quince. "How long does that take to walk?"

"Oh, about half an hour."

Timothy relieved Rose of Prue, and Rose took Regan's arm. She was in high spirits and, of course, could not experience any of the apprehensions that were troubling the Antigeosians. "Gosh, we're really here!" she whispered. "Back on the Earth and in England! I still can't believe it. . . ."

Now there was enough light for them to be able to make out the ridge of hills beyond Brydd and to the east was the sea, a level streak of grey against the paleness of the dawn. They passed Luggy Martin's cottage and Regan caught her breath. It was an ugly and dilapidated cottage. Many of its windows had been patched with squares of cardboard and the whole building looked as if it were about to collapse under the weight of its thatch. "A house?" she whispered, and Rose laughed.

"Of a sort," she said. "A cottage, actually."

"And humans live in it?"

"Yes, but not all houses are like that. That's a particularly decrepit one."

When they reached the outskirts of Brydd, Regan once more became conscious of movement behind them. "There's someone!" she breathed, and swung round to see a human gliding along the road towards them on a weird machine with two wheels.

The others stopped and Pollenport remarked that they had better brazen it out. "I'd hoped that we could get to the Coxes without being seen," he said, "but it can't be helped."

Then he raised his voice and spoke to the man on the bicycle, who dismounted. Regan drew back nervously, and Rose was not altogether surprised. Had she had any say in the matter she would never have chosen Luggy Martin to be the first human being that Regan would meet on the Earth. He looked as if he had recently crawled out of a hole in the ground. He was grimy and unkempt and the front of his waterproof jacket was thick with mud. Huge ears stood out at right-angles to his head and a week's growth of beard covered his narrow chin. He had a predatory look about him, and when he opened his mouth to speak Rose was not surprised to see that he had fangs rather than teeth—yellow pointed fangs, like a wolf's.

He told them that the Coxes had their shop in the Square, then hastily mounted his bicycle and pedalled away. "We could have dispensed with that little encounter," muttered Pollenport. "Now I suppose the news will be all over Brydd in no time."

"What was he?" asked Regan, in a whisper.

"Just a man," said Rose, "but you won't see many like him."

"Does he kill people?"

Rose smiled. "I don't expect so. What do you mean?"

"But you told me there were some people, called soldiers, who kill other people?"

"Oh, I see. . . . No, they don't look like that, and anyway they're quite safe to meet. I'll try and explain later on."

As they walked through the deserted streets towards the Square, Quince and Regan fell silent, gazing about them, and Rose tried to imagine how a small English town would strike creatures who had never before seen a building and whose only idea of a habitation was an underground one. They came to a church and Regan stared wonderingly at it, but refrained from asking Rose what it was, realising, perhaps, that it was one of the many things that could not be explained in a couple of sentences. Then, in the churchyard, she saw trees for the first time and hastily lowered her eyes. Rose smiled, remembering that in the Antigean view trees were not decent, and for a few moments Regan's embarrassment was comparable with a nineteenth-century lady missionary's on first encountering naked savages.

"This must be the Square," said Pollenport, as they turned a corner. "Ah, yes, and there's the Coxes' shop."

They stood in a little group outside the shop and Pollenport rang the bell, keeping his finger on the bell-push for nearly a minute. They heard someone move in the room above the shop and then a window was thrown up.

"Hullo?" said a sleepy voice.

"Digby Cox?"

The young man who was gazing down at them seemed hardly awake. "No, Bryan Cox," he said. "What do you want?"

"Well, I'm Jonah Pollenport and——"

Bryan's yelp of astonishment ran round the Square like a shot. "What? Pollenport . . . Crumbs!"

He withdrew his head so quickly that he struck it on the bottom of the window, but he didn't seem to notice it, and a moment later they heard him shouting to his brother. "Digby! . . . For God's sake—Digby!"

He let them in without troubling to put on a dressing-gown over his pyjamas and it occurred to Rose that he was almost convinced it was all a dream.

"God, Professor Pollenport!" he cried, pumping Pollenport's arm. "Then you survived! And how the deuce did you get here? . . . Look, come into the kitchen. It's warmer than anywhere else, and I'll make some coffee."

And it was at that point that Regan started to enjoy herself. She liked the Coxes' kitchen. She liked its flowered curtains and the check tablecloth, and the idea of people preparing and cooking their own food amused her.

Digby Cox came in, still struggling to tie the cord of his dressing-gown. "What's going on?" he asked, and as he gazed round at his queerly-garbed guests it was clear that he hadn't an idea who they were.

Bryan swung round from the gas-stove. "Digby, it's Professor Pollenport and the others from the spaceship!" he said. "God knows how they got here, but here they are and I'm making some coffee."

Digby could hardly speak. "And the spaceship?" he asked, in a weak voice.

"We've just disembarked from it," said Pollenport. "Out on the Marsh."

"Good Lord! And it's still out there?"

"No, it's taken off again and we've come on ahead, as ambassadors, as it were. In the circumstances, we decided that you were the first people we ought to see."

Rose said: "Mr. Cox, is there a bed I could put Prue into? She'll probably sleep for hours."

"Yes, she can have my bed," said Digby. "I'll show you the way."

Rose took Prue from Timothy and followed Digby up the stairs. "You know," he said over his shoulder, "this is all so fantastic that I don't know where to begin." They went into the bedroom. "Anyway, there's a bed for Prue and you'll join us in the kitchen when you've settled her, will you?"

Rose thanked him, then managed to get Prue's tunic off almost without waking her. Leggings and shoes followed the tunic, but when Rose put the child into the bed Prue opened her eyes. "What is this, Mummy?" she asked.

"It's called a bed," Rose told her, "and it's for sleeping in. You'll have one of your own soon."

"It's funny, isn't it?"

Rose kissed her. "When you wake up and find yourself in a strange place you'll remember not to be frightened, won't you?"

"Yes. Where will you be?"

"Only a little way away, and if you call me I'll hear you."

"All right."

Rose kissed her again, tucked her up and went to the window. It was almost full daylight now and the mist was rising. She gazed down at the little garden and at the backs of the other houses and suddenly felt almost weak with happiness. She was home, she was in England, she had travelled farther than any other woman had ever travelled and now she was home. A sleek black cat was walking along the wall at the bottom of the garden and she wished she was near enough to stroke it. It was five years since she had spoken to a cat or stroked one, and now she decided that at the first opportunity she must get a kitten.

She went back to the kitchen and found that Pollenport was in the midst of explaining his deception. Bryan was still at the stove, but all the others were sitting at the table with cups of coffee in front of them. Regan was tasting hers and Rose asked her in a whisper what she thought of it. "Do you like it?" she asked.

"I think so," said Regan doubtfully. "Yes, I think so; but I don't understand how it ever occurred to anyone to drink it in the first place. It's not like anything we drink on Antigeos, is it?"

Rose laughed, and she could see that Regan was even more puzzled by the cigarette that Digby Cox was smoking. . . .

"Well, that's the story," Pollenport was saying. "I won't dot all the i's or cross all the t's just now, because I feel that we mustn't let grass grow under our feet. I think we should be discussing what happens next."

Digby nodded. "Yes, and I think the first thing we should do is contact Jim Dawson on the *Post*. That newspaper is on our side, as it were, and I feel it's most important that your story gets the right presentation. If the public can be made to see that you were forced to take the line you took, they'll condone the deception, but if not, not. Anyway, that's how I feel about it."

"All right. Then you telephone this Jim Dawson, and

then perhaps we can arrange to meet him in London. Has he a flat, do you know?"

"Yes."

"Then perhaps we could meet him there. Naturally, we don't want to appear too publicly until we've acquired some different clothes."

"Yes, that's a point," agreed Digby. "I think Bryan and I between us can probably manage to fix Timothy up with something wearable, but I doubt if we've got anything that would fit you or Quince. And then there are the girls."

"Yes," said Rose, "and we intend to have fun. Do you know I haven't had a dress of my own for five years?"

Digby laughed and assured her that she was looking very chic as she was, then he looked back at Pollenport. "Well, Professor," he went on, "I suggest that when I phone Jim I'd better ask him to get someone along from one of the big stores to take your measurements and get you fixed up. By the way, we've a car, so the journey to London presents no great problems."

"Fine," said Pollenport, "and while I think of it, I might as well tell you that we haven't arrived without a penny to our names."

He put his hand inside his tunic and produced a small slab of gold. It was about the size of a shilling bar of chocolate and he handed it to Digby. "Gold," he said. "We've quite a number of those ingots on the space-ship."

Bryan whirled round. "Christmas!" he exclaimed. "I want to touch it!"

Mystified, Regan glanced at Rose. "But you have gold on the Earth?" she asked.

"Yes," said Rose. "But not in lumps. Or at least what lumps there are we keep in holes in the ground."

"Oh dear," sighed Regan. "I'll never understand."

Digby handed the ingot back to Pollenport and got up. "I'll go and ring Jim," he said, and went through into the shop. . . .

III

A bell rang in the servants' hall at Narraway Towers and Davidson scowled and pushed his tea-cup away from him. "Now what does old Worry-guts want?" he muttered, as he carefully nipped out his half-smoked cigarette and put it in his waistcoat pocket. "Can't even have breakfast in peace now." He passed a hand over his face and got up. "He ought to see a psychiatrist, really he ought. Paranoia, that's his trouble."

"Actually, you're making a little mistake," said Cook, and pointed up to the tell-tale. "He didn't ring. It's the front door."

"Oh, a caller. Well, what's the difference? I still can't have my breakfast in peace."

A flight of stairs led down to the hall and the front door and, as Davidson descended, he glanced out of a little window set in the turn of the stairs. A shabby lorry was drawn up at the door and standing on the step were two rough-looking men whom Davidson found it easy to disapprove of. "The front door?" he murmured. "I'll give them front door!"

He gave his waistcoat a tug, threw back his head and opened the door. He sniffed loudly, and then, gazing down upon Bob Hancock and Luggy Martin with all the disdain at his command, asked them to state their business.

"Mr. Davidson, isn't it?" said old Hancock, ingratiatingly. "You remember I come here before? With

159

that wireless thing from Brydd. Well, the fact is we've got important information for his lordship."

Davidson preserved a non-committal silence and Hancock looked uneasily from him to Luggy. "That's right, isn't it, Cousin Charles?" he said.

"'Sright," muttered Luggy, staring down at his Wellingtons.

"What information?" asked Davidson.

"Well, I think we ought to see his lordship in person," said Hancock.

"Oh, you do, do you? I suppose you think his lordship ought to hold himself available to every Tom, Dick or Harry whose hen has laid a treble-yolked egg? Is that what you think?"

"No, of course not, but this is real unusual information. To do with the spaceship."

"'Sright," said Luggy, suddenly raising his shifty gaze. "It come down. It come down on the Marsh. I seen it, and I seen the folk what got out of it. Yes, and I spoke to 'em, and two of 'em weren't human beings. They wanted to know the way to the Coxes' wireless shop."

Davidson stiffened. "Are you trying to tell me that a spaceship landed at Brydd this morning?"

"'Sright," said Luggy. "It took off again, but it landed all right. I seen it."

Davidson gazed at both the men for a moment, then withdrew. "Wait there," he said, and as he mounted the stairs he rapidly considered a number of ways in which he might turn this startling information to his own profit. None of them, however, was immediately practicable, and he decided that there was nothing for it but to pass on the information to his employer.

Lord Sanderlake had finished his breakfast and was steadily ploughing his way through the morning's newspapers.

160

"Good morning, my lord," said Davidson. "It appears that a spaceship has landed at Brydd."

Lord Sanderlake jumped a foot and swung round. "What's that? What's that you're saying?"

"A spaceship, my lord. At Brydd. There are two yokels at the door and they've just come over from Brydd with the information. One of them claims to have actually seen the spaceship with his own eyes."

"You mean, a spaceship from Antigeos?"

"I'm afraid, my lord, that I have no information as to its port of origin, but it appears that a handful of people disembarked from the machine and made their way to Mr. Digby Cox's place of business."

Lord Sanderlake turned pale and his hand shook. "I'll have to see these two men," he said. "Ask them to come up."

Davidson was unable to contrive to stay in the morning-room during the interview, and so he returned thoughtfully to the servants' hall.

"Who was it?" asked Cook.

"A couple of louts with red-hot news for the *Messenger*. Their hen has laid an egg with three yolks."

"That's nothing," said Cook. "Why, I've handled an egg with six yolks, all fertile. I hope you sent them packing."

"On the contrary. Old Worry-guts is now interviewing them, and I've no doubt that their story will make the front page."

"Well, I don't know," said Cook, then glanced at him with a dawning suspicion. "Or are you pulling my leg?"

"Heaven forbid, and now perhaps I can have a cup of tea and a cigarette in peace."

He had just finished the cigarette when Lord Sanderlake rang for him and he lost no time in answering the summons.

"Davidson, show these gentlemen to the small study," said Lord Sanderlake. "I'm arranging for a reporter to come down and interview them. Then come back to me here."

Davidson, deeply experienced in his employer's moods, knew that a crisis was impending, and he responded with a sense of heightened nervous tension. He took Hancock and Luggy to the small study and, as he closed the door on them, made an effort to marshal his thoughts. He felt he stood on the brink of momentous events, yet he could not imagine what those events might be, and neither could he sense whether they would be advantageous to him or the reverse. It was strange, that feeling of mounting tension, and it put Davidson in mind of a violin string tuned to breaking point.

His employer was speaking to the *Messenger* office on the private line when Davidson returned to the morning-room, instructing the news-editor to send along a reporter and a photographer to get Luggy Martin's story. "And when they've finished here they'd better go on to Brydd," he said, then put his hand over the mouthpiece and spoke to Davidson.

"Get me Mr. Keble-Keith," he murmured, pointing to the other telephone. "He'll probably still be at his flat and you'll have to look it up in the book."

Keble-Keith was a sore point with Davidson and at the sound of the name his nerves screamed as if they'd been touched with hot irons. Keble-Keith had made a monkey out of him, had swindled him out of five thousand pounds, and many nights Davidson's hatred and resentment had kept him awake into the early hours; and three o'clock in the morning had often found him planning elaborate and ghastly forms of revenge upon Mr. Keble-Keith. He was a vengeful man, and it was his belief that no one could make a monkey out of him and get away with it indefinitely.

He found the telephone-number in the directory and the financier himself answered the call. The muscles of Davidson's jaw tightened when he heard his enemy's voice, and he had difficulty in controlling his own. "Mr. Keble-Keith? Lord Sanderlake wishes to speak to you."

He put down the receiver and went through the motions of straightening the newspapers until Lord Sanderlake had finished speaking on the other line. He did not mean to miss anything if he could help it, and he was relieved when presently his employer finished on one telephone and moved to the other without so much as glancing at him.

"Keble-Keith? . . . Look, an amazing thing's happened, and I've got to see you right away. . . . It seems that Pollenport and his crowd have just landed at Brydd. . . . What? . . . No, apparently it wasn't destroyed. I suppose it was a trick, damn them. . . . Yes. . . . But, good God, you can't take that attitude! . . . But, damn it, my dear fellow, the whole idea stemmed from you in the first place. . . . Look, if you think you can put me out on a limb you've got another think coming, and I've got to talk to you. . . . What? . . . All right. . . . Yes. . . . Very well, I'll be with you within the hour. Good-bye."

He slammed the receiver down with a bad grace and glanced at Davidson. "Tell Breen to bring the car round," he snapped. "I want to leave for London in ten minutes' time."

"Very good, my lord."

As Davidson left the room, his face was dark with concentrated thought and the muscles of his jaw twitched nervously. He went to the house-telephone in the passage and was about to ring the garage when he had second thoughts, and it was on that change of decision that everything else, the whole strange course of that strange day, was to depend.

He left the house by a side door and headed for the garage. The Rolls-Royce, freshly washed and polished, stood in the yard, and the door that led to Breen's flat above the garage stood open. Davidson tapped on it perfunctorily and started up the stairs. "Wally?" he called.

"Yes, come in, Bob. I'm just having a cup of tea. Want one?"

"No, thanks."

Davidson went into the flat's tiny sitting-room, where the chauffeur sat at a table with a newspaper spread out in front of him. "Wally, old Worry-guts wants the car——" he began, but Breen interrupted him.

"Bob, are you all right?" he asked. "You look awful."

"What do you mean?"

"Why, you look sort of grey and—well, I don't know. You don't look good, anyhow."

"I'm all right, but the point is that the old man wants to go up to town."

"On a Saturday? What's come over him?"

"I don't know, but what I do know is that I've got a special reason for wanting to go up too. Woman-trouble, and I've *got* to go up. What's it worth to you, Wally?"

"What, you mean you want me to swing the lead?"

Davidson nodded. "I'll give you a quid," he said, and took out his wallet.

"Oh, I'll do it for love and be glad of the rest," said Breen. "I'm easy. Better say it's a chill on the stomach, because I've had a go of that before."

"Well, thanks a lot, Wally," said Davidson and, hating to be under an obligation to anyone, insisted on Breen having the pound. . . .

He did things that morning without knowing why he did them. A bleak sort of excitement gripped him and he felt like a gambler who knows he must lose, yet cannot refrain from playing. He drove the car round to the front of the house, and came upon Lord Sanderlake putting his overcoat on in the hall.

"I regret to say, my lord, that Breen's on the sick list," said Davidson. "A gastric upset, I fear."

"Damn," muttered Lord Sanderlake. "I suppose we'll have to get someone from the village."

"Yes, my lord. Unless you'd like me to drive you."

Lord Sanderlake gave him a grateful glance. "Well, I know you don't like acting as chauffeur," he said, "but I should be most extraordinarily glad if you would."

"Certainly, my lord: I'll go and change, but I won't be five minutes."

He ascended the stairs and outside his employer's bedroom he hesitated for a couple of seconds, then quietly opened the door and went in. It was as if he were controlled by an agency outside himself, and he went to the night-table beside Lord Sanderlake's bed and opened its drawer. He glanced nervously over his shoulder, then took a small automatic from the drawer and dropped it into his trousers' pocket. After that he went along to his own room, to change. . . .

IV

Keble-Keith's flat was as unpretentious as his clothes and it had something of the same air of shabbiness. It was on the ground floor of an old-fashioned block off Baker Street, and Keble-Keith lived without servants except for a daily woman who came in in the late afternoon, cleaned the place, then cooked an evening meal for him. He cooked his own breakfast, and in fact he had been doing so when Lord Sanderlake telephoned him.

Oddly enough, the news of the spaceship's arrival did not come entirely as a surprise to him. He had half-imagined that something of the sort might happen. He had a devious mind and was given to suspecting deception in any activities that involved human beings, and now he could see clearly that the time had come for him to dissociate himself from the *Daily Messenger*. He surmised that there was now going to be an unholy row, and he wanted no part of the anxieties that were necessarily troubling Lord Sanderlake.

He was smiling faintly as he left the telephone and went back to the serious business of getting his breakfast. He took his egg out of its saucepan, popped it into an egg-cup and cracked its top firmly. All in all, he reflected, things had turned out very satisfactorily. It was true that his greatest dream, the colonisation of Antigeos, was probably as far away from realisation as ever, but meanwhile he had made a great deal of money. He had started by selling a large block of Anglo-Antigean to Lord Sanderlake at an enormous profit, and he had held on to another block while awaiting events. The shares rose steeply when the news of Antigeos broke, and he had sold at the top of the market immediately on learning of the Coxes' treachery. In fact, he had sold far more shares than he held—at eighty-three shillings a share—then the bottom had dropped out of the market and he had cleaned up. Anglo-Antigeans now stood at nine shillings and no doubt would drop still farther before he had to deliver. It was all very satisfactory, and he saw no reason why he should now involve himself in Lord Sanderlake's troubles. . . .

He finished his breakfast, exchanged his dressing-gown for a jacket, and by the time Lord Sanderlake called he was sitting composedly in front of the fire reading *The Times*. As he had expected, the newspaper-proprietor was in a highly nervous state and he was hardly in the flat before he asked Keble-Keith what he thought should be done. "By God," he said, "we've certainly got to keep our end up, or we're for it."

Keble-Keith helped him off with his coat and shepherded him into the living-room. "Well, Lord Sanderlake," he said, "as I told you on the telephone, I don't see quite how I come into it, but, of course, if it's just advice that you want——"

Lord Sanderlake snorted and, sitting down, gazed at his host uneasily. "What do you mean, you don't come into it?" he asked. "It was your scheme, your plan, your idea."

"Perhaps, but you were under no compulsion to adopt it. In any case, that's all water under the bridge, and now, with the best will in the world, I just don't see how I can help."

Lord Sanderlake jerked a cigar from his case and bit off its end. "In other words, you're taking a run-out powder? Is that it?"

"No, of course not. Surely you know me too well to think that. But what can I do? Or perhaps first you might explain exactly what the trouble is?"

Lord Sanderlake put a match to his cigar and glared balefully through the smoke. "The trouble, Mr. Keble-Keith, is this," he said, in tones that were unnaturally calm. "You and I between us concocted a war-scare. We led the public to believe that the Antigeosians were about to invade us and we demanded total mobilisation. Well, the Coxes somewhat upset our project and the only thing that enabled us to survive at that point was the news of the spaceship's destruction. It distracted the public and in any case no one could say which version of events was the correct one—ours or the *Daily Post's*. Now, however, it's a different story. Pollenport is here. So are the Antigeosians. Pollenport will make the truth known by means of newspaper articles, radio broadcasts, television broadcasts, and when the public learns how very nearly it was tricked into war it will set up a howl for blood. . . . My blood, Mr. Keble-Keith, and your blood. And no matter how reluctant the Government may be to act in the matter, it will be forced to by public opinion, it will have to find scapegoats, and we can guess where it will look for them. I haven't had time yet to consider what the legal aspect may be, but clearly we can be charged with causing a public mischief, and there may be graver charges, Mr. Keble-Keith—far graver charges."

"I think you're probably exaggerating," said Keble-Keith, "but I'm still interested to know how you think I can help. Have you any concrete suggestions?"

"Yes, I have a suggestion," said Lord Sanderlake, "and I'll tell you what it is. You've got an ultra-short-wave receiving set, haven't you?"

For a moment Keble-Keith looked considerably surprised. Then he remembered his earlier deception and decided to hold his peace.

"Haven't you?" asked Lord Sanderlake. "Because you told me you had, and my idea is that we concoct a whole series of messages alleged to have been received on that set. Messages purporting to come from Antigeos, but on a different wave-length from that used by Pollenport. We can argue that we picked them up in good faith, and that it wasn't until now, with Pollenport's arrival, that we realised we'd been hoaxed. As far as the hoaxer is concerned, presumably he was some irresponsible young radio amateur who amused himself by picking up Pollenport's transmissions, perverting them and then re-transmitting them on a different wave-length. . . . Well, that's not a brilliant suggestion, but it's all I can offer and it might provide just the type of smoke-screen we need. And, as you can see, I shall want your co-operation with it."

"Yes," said Keble-Keith, with the ghost of a smile. "And the only snag is that I haven't a receiving set."

"You mean, you lied to me?"

"Yes, I did," said Keble-Keith, easily. "Yes, I lied to you, Lord Sanderlake."

The newspaper-proprietor went red. "Then how the devil did you discover that I was in communication with Pollenport?" he asked.

Keble-Keith's smile grew a little more marked. "I see no reason why I shouldn't tell you," he said. "The truth is that one of your employees sold me the information."

"Sold it you? Who?"

"I think his name was Davidson. Anyway, he's your butler."

Lord Sanderlake choked, and the redness of his face took on a purple tint. "My God, I can't believe that," he said, in a strangled voice. "Why, Davidson's been with me for thirty years! He has many faults, but I've never had cause to question his loyalty. No, I don't believe it!"

"And yet it's true," murmured Keble-Keith, almost wistfully.

"How much did you pay him?"

"Let me see—unless my memory's at fault, I gave him a cheque for five thousand."

"Nonsense!" roared Lord Sanderlake. "If he'd touched that kind of money, I know damn-well that I'd have had an inkling of it. Why, when an aunt left him a couple of hundred he was drunk for a week."

Then he mystified Keble-Keith by suddenly jumping up and going to the window. The Rolls-Royce stood outside with Davidson at the wheel, and now Lord Sanderlake threw the window up. "Davidson!" he yelled. "I want you a moment. . . ."

For the first time that morning, Keble-Keith was visibly disconcerted. "You mean, you've got the man with you?" he asked, as Lord Sanderlake withdrew his head and let the curtains fall back into place.

"Yes, I have. He's driving me."

"Well, I think it's a little unnecessary to have him in here."

"Oh, you do, do you? That's very interesting!"

The door-bell rang and Lord Sanderlake strode out into the hall. "Come in, Davidson," he said, as he opened the door. "There are a couple of questions I want to ask you."

Davidson followed Lord Sanderlake into the front room, and Keble-Keith, sitting forward in his chair and gazing into the fire, did not look up. The newspaper-proprietor hesitated before he put his question and for some reason it seemed to him that Davidson was looking more solid and saturnine than ever. He was wearing a navy-blue mackintosh, belted, and he had a hand in one of its pockets. His eyes were unnaturally dark, as if he had atropine in them, and they were as expressionless as pools of ink.

Lord Sanderlake cleared his throat. "Now look here, Davidson," he said, "Mr. Keble-Keith tells me that he paid you five thousand pounds in return for certain information. Is that so?"

If Davidson heard him, he gave no sign of it. He was staring at Keble-Keith and there was tension about the muscles of his face that Lord Sanderlake found alarming. Then he drew his hand from his pocket and two seconds ticked by before the newspaper magnate realised it was gripping an automatic.

He gasped: "Davidson!" and, as Keble-Keith's head jerked up, Davidson fired.

The bullet hit the financier neatly in the temple, rocking him sideways, so that he slumped over the chair's farther arm. Blood trickled darkly from the wound, and Davidson swung round, pointing the gun at his employer. "Sit down, Worry-guts!" he barked. "And keep away from that telephone."

"But, Davidson——"

"Shut up! And sit down . . ."

Lord Sanderlake sat down and his face was ashen. Davidson leant over the dead man and placed the gun in his hand, pushing the index finger through the trigger-guard and curling the other fingers round the butt. He took great care about this, and not until he was entirely satisfied did he stand back and survey his handiwork.

Then he turned to Lord Sanderlake. "We're going to wait here five minutes," he said, "and if anyone heard the shot they'll be here by then. If that happens, you'll be dialling nine-nine-nine and your story is that he shot himself before you could stop him, and you called me in right away. If no one shows up within five minutes, we clear out and it will be assumed that he shot himself soon after you left."

Lord Sanderlake clutched the arms of his chair and struggled to speak. "Don't be an idiot, Davidson!" he gasped at length. "You can't make me an accessory! I'll have to report this to——"

"You'll be a fool if you do," said Davidson, coldly. "For one thing, that pistol's yours——"

"What?"

"Yes, it's yours. It's the one that is normally by your bed at Narraway Towers, but I'm the only one who could swear to it. Why, I bought it for you. In Rome. That time you had a nasty attack of the willies and thought there were Reds under the bed. It wasn't declared at the Customs, and you don't hold a licence for it, so you're all right as long as you do as I tell you. It was suicide, see, and if you've got any sense you'll be the last person to start hinting at murder. You had a motive for wanting him dead, and I had none—none that the police could find out about, anyway. Why, even if I confessed to the job they'd merely think I was trying to shield you. And now, thanks to me, you're sitting pretty."

Lord Sanderlake moistened his dry lips. "What do you mean?" he croaked.

"The spaceship landing put you in a spot, didn't it? Didn't it?"

"Yes."

"Well, now you're not in a spot any longer. Your story can be that Keble-Keith, as managing director of Anglo-Antigean, had been supplying you with news from Antigeos. He claimed to have an ultra-short-wave receiving set, and you believed him. He gave you a lot more information than the Coxes gave you, because he claimed to have been on the job much longer, he claimed to have been getting messages long before Pollenport and his pals got taken prisoner. That, he told you, was how he came to know the truth about the Antigean intentions—that they were belligerent. All right, and then this morning you hear about Pollenport's arrival and all your doubts about Keble-Keith's good faith come to a head. So you come along here and tackle him, and he, realising that it can only be a matter of hours before the whole swindle's exposed, shoots himself."

Lord Sanderlake looked uneasily at the corpse, then back again at Davidson. "Why did you do it?" he mumbled.

"That's something you'll never know, Worry-guts," said Davidson, "but I'll tell you that if you hadn't called me I'd have come here anyway. I worked it all out while I was sitting in the car, and it all went just as I planned it. Oh, and by the way, this is only an interlude. To-morrow you'll find me just as good a butler as ever I was and you just won't know the difference—except that you'll never be able to fire me."

Lord Sanderlake shivered, and Davidson glanced at his watch. "Come on," he said. "The five minutes are up!"

He held open the door for his employer and followed him to the car.

"Where to, my lord?" he asked with a return to his usual voice and manner.

"I don't know. I suppose—the *Messenger* building."

V

In Jim Dawson's flat, bedlam reigned. It was an extremely small flat, in a Chelsea square, and at one period of the morning it contained no fewer than sixteen people. Not since the cabin scene in *A Night at the Opera* had so many people been crowded into so small a space, and the chaos was comparable. Sasha-lights flashed and flickered, and in one corner of the room Jim Dawson hammered out his story of the space-travellers' arrival while Deborah read it over the telephone as he wrote it, transmitting it to the *Evening*

Post's news-room. Prue was now fully awake and the excitement had gone to her head, and now she was tearing from room to room, squealing like a stuck steam-whistle.

Tailors busied themselves with Pollenport, Timothy and Quince, and dressmakers occupied themselves with Rose and Regan, and the photographers kept crying, "Now please, just one more in native dress before you change . . ." and Digby and Bryan saw to the catering, making innumerable cups of tea and cutting innumerable sandwiches.

By two o'clock the worst of the turmoil had subsided and the lull gave opportunity for surveying the field and reckoning gains. The photographers had retreated and so had the tailors and dressmakers. The floor of the flat was littered with shallow boxes that had, until recently, contained shirts, vests and pants, and a variety of women's underclothing, and now the six from Antigeos were dressed in terrestrial fashion. Quince had on a Lovat tweed jacket and was wearing trousers for the first time in his life. Timothy, in a green gabardine suit, was looking rather spectacular, while Pollenport, more conservative, had plumped for dark grey worsted. Cirrus skirts, or a modification of them, were still the fashion and both the girls wore them. Rose's was pale blue and Regan's was bronze, and Rose had learned that the deep-vee neckline was a thing of the past. Now bodices fitted the figure but had high stiffened collars and were sleeveless. Prue had on a white shirt and shorts, and the pockets in the shorts both puzzled and fascinated her. "What are they for?" she asked.

"You can keep things in them," said Rose, and Digby took a sixpenny piece out of his pocket.

"Here you are, Prue," he said. "You can put this in one of your pockets for a start."

"Thank you," said Prue, and examined the coin gravely. "What does it do?"

"You can buy things with it," Digby told her, but when Rose tried to elucidate the statement for Prue's understanding she met with very little success. It was clear that Prue was going to find the economic ways of this strange new world just as mysterious as Quince and Regan found them.

Jim Dawson came to the end of a long telephone conversation and now asked Pollenport if he could have a word with him.

"Of course," murmured Pollenport, and followed Jim into the bedroom.

"I've just been talking to the editor-in-chief," said Jim, "and he's got various messages for you. He wants to meet you as soon as possible, and so does Sir Hew Buchanan, who is the chairman of our Board of Trustees. He asked me to emphasise that he's not trying to make a newspaper stunt out of you and the spaceship, and all the rest of it."

"Thank God for that," said Pollenport. "One way and another I think I've suffered enough from Fleet Street, in both the recent and the more distant past, to last me a lifetime. Of course I'll meet him. And Sir Hew. In fact, I'll be happy to go along with you just as soon as you're ready."

"Good. And he also hopes you'll spend your first week in London as guests of the *Evening Post*. If you're agreeable, I'm to try and get the pent-house suite at the Barchester for you."

Pollenport was inclined to accept, but felt it might be better to reserve his decision until later. "Let's go along to Fleet Street," he said, "and see what your editor and Sir Hew have to say."

They emerged from the bedroom to find that the

others were planning a tour of London in the Coxes' car. "Any objections, Daddy?" asked Rose.

"Well, no, but for Heaven's sake be discreet. Remember that the news of the spaceship landing will be out by now, and if Regan and Quince get recognised you'll be mobbed. What are you going to do about their antennæ?"

"Regan can wear a scarf over her head, and we've got a hat for Quince."

"Yes," said Timothy, "but he doesn't like wearing it. He says it's worse than being deaf and almost as bad as being blind."

"It's true, Jonah," said Quince. "Must I wear it? You see, Regan and I are finding the patterns of London's movement almost the most fascinating thing about it."

"Still, you'd better wear it," said Pollenport. "Nothing like you two has ever happened to London before and the excitement promises to be tremendous. Later on, of course, it will be different."

"All right, Jonah," said Quince, and ruefully placed the hat on his head. It was a wide-brimmed, high-crowned trilby, and there was plenty of room under it for his antennæ, but wearing it he looked so miserable that Pollenport almost relented. In fact, Quince looked like a small boy who had been invited to a party with the strict injunction that he mustn't eat anything. . . .

Jim Dawson drove Pollenport to Fleet Street in his monstrous car, and the *Daily Post's* editor-in-chief turned out to be a very fat and rather nondescript man with a rubbery smile and an automatically genial manner. Pollenport was not much impressed by him, but Sir Hew Buchanan was another matter altogether. He was a tall, grave, long-faced Scotsman and, although he had probably never seen a joke in his life, he had considerable charm and was doubtless no fool. He somehow managed to give the impression that his newspapers were really a side-line and that his real interests lay on a higher plane. One felt that very little happened in official circles without his approval and nothing without his knowledge, and Pollenport was not surprised to learn that within the hour he had been speaking with the Prime Minister.

"As no doubt you know, Professor Pollenport," said Sir Hew, "a certain amount of confusion obtains in the public mind as regards the Antigeosians' intentions, and the Prime Minister thinks it essential that the misunderstanding should be cleared up as soon as possible."

"Of course," murmured Pollenport.

"And you have absolutely no doubt as to the friendliness of the Antigeosians?"

"None whatsoever, Sir Hew. They haven't a word for war in their language, and they have such a loathing of violence that anything in the way of aggressive action would be impossible for them."

"I see. Then what do you think Lord Sanderlake's motives were in so misrepresenting their visit?"

Pollenport told him at some length, and as Sir Hew listened his face grew longer and graver. He put the tips of his fingers together as if he were praying for Lord Sanderlake's soul, and shook his head sadly. There was silence for some minutes when Pollenport finished speaking, then Sir Hew passed a long bony hand over his face.

"Thank you, Professor Pollenport," he murmured, "and I can see that there's much to be said for your case. Aye, it will be a verra serious matter for Lord Sanderlake when the facts are put before the Public Prosecutor."

"I suppose so."

"And where, Professor Pollenport, is the spaceship now?"

"It's standing about a thousand miles off the Earth, waiting to hear from me that the coast is clear. You see, I've various credentials from the Antigean authorities addressed to the terrestrial Heads of State, and I'm hoping that I shan't have much difficulty in establishing the visitors' good faith. For instance, do you think the Prime Minister will see me?"

"I'm sairtain of it," said Sir Hew, and with a quick movement reached for the telephone and pulled it towards him. . . .

VI

At a single stroke Davidson had acquired the power of life or death over his master, yet, almost in the moment of acquiring it, he made a strange and important discovery. He discovered that he did not want anything drastic to happen to old Worry-guts. He did not want any revolutionary change in the *status quo*. For years he had carried on a subdued, yet none the less relentless, bullying of his master, and now it had reached a logical climax all that he wished was that the position should be indefinitely maintained. The truth was that it was only as Lord Sanderlake's butler that he felt himself to have any reality.

Meanwhile, he was determined not to let the newspaper-proprietor out of his sight until they were back at Narraway Towers. Lord Sanderlake was in a highly volatile state and he was not to be trusted. Not for another twenty-four hours or so would he really appreciate the finer points of the position, and in the meantime he might very well attempt to contact Scotland Yard in the hope of getting Davidson charged with Keble-Keith's murder. As yet he did not fully understand how near was his own neck to the noose.

"My God, Davidson, what are we to do?" he wailed when they reached his office at the *Messenger* building. "There must be something!"

"I would suggest, my lord, that we return to Narraway Towers and take it easy. If there is to be any trouble, it will find your lordship all right without your lordship having to look for it——"

Dora Nutt came in with a sheaf of letters and Lord Sanderlake scowled. "No, I'm not to be disturbed, Dora," he snapped. "I only came in on account of this spaceship nonsense, and everything else can wait till Monday!"

"Very well, Lord Sanderlake."

Then the newspaper-proprietor had what he thought was a flash of inspiration and stopped Dora on her way to the door. "Get Mr. Keble-Keith on the telephone," he said. "He'll probably be at his flat."

"Yes, Lord Sanderlake."

As she left them, Davidson shook his head reprovingly. "Highly unnecessary, my lord," he murmured. "I do suggest that your lordship tries to avoid forcing the issue."

"Oh, for God's sake let me handle things in my own way!" growled Lord Sanderlake. "The sooner we can get the news of Keble-Keith's suicide made public, the better it will be for me. Later in the day I intend to seek an interview with the Prime Minister, and he'll be far more inclined to believe my story if by then he knows about the suicide."

"Ah, but I very much doubt if the Prime Minister will see your lordship," said Davidson, and Lord Sanderlake glanced up sharply.

"What the devil do you know about it?" he asked. "The P.M.'s an old friend of mine. Of course he'll see me. God, man, he's never ceased to be grateful to me for my services in helping break the rail strike of '66."

Davidson merely looked deferential and said nothing, and just then Dora Nutt returned with the news that there was no reply from Keble-Keith's flat. "I've also rung his office," she said, "and they say they're not expecting him in today."

"Well, keep ringing the flat until you get a reply!"

"Yes, Lord Sanderlake, but you don't think he may be away for the week-end?"

"No, I don't. I was with him less than an hour ago, and if he were going away he'd have mentioned it. Keep ringing him."

The strange feeling of nervous tension that had gripped Davidson earlier that morning had eased off with Keble-Keith's death, but now it was returning. The muscles of his face twitched and more than anything he wished that his employer would have the sense to return to Narraway Towers. He felt as if disaster impended, and an inner voice told him that it was dangerous to remain in London. Then a heavy object thudded to the floor of the office and he jumped involuntarily.

"What's that, my lord?"

Lord Sanderlake jerked his head towards the pneumatic conveyor, and Davidson saw that beneath it lay a large cylindrical container. "The evening papers," explained his employer. "They come up throughout the day. Let's have a look at them."

Davidson fetched the container and opened it. The *Evening Post* was the only paper to interest Lord Sanderlake and its headline was a typographical shout:

THE SPACESHIP LANDS!

So far the story that followed was brief, and Lord Sanderlake was not surprised to learn that the six who had disembarked from the spaceship were heading for London. *Later editions will carry full and exclusive interviews and photographs* promised the *Post*.

Lord Sanderlake growled with frustration. "My story," he grunted, "and they've scooped it! None of this would have happened, but for Keble-Keith! My God, I could murd——" He broke off hastily, and blew his nose to cover his confusion.

Dora came in to say that there was still definitely no reply from Keble-Keith's flat. "Shall I send a messenger round?" she asked.

Lord Sanderlake considered the suggestion for a moment, then nodded. "Yes, do that, Dora," he said. "To be perfectly frank, I'm getting a little bit worried. When I left him this morning he was in a somewhat sombre mood. . . . Yes, send a messenger along, and if he gets no answer tell him to telephone me."

Old Worry-guts was taking it too fast, Davidson reflected, but if things went wrong, well, it would be his own funeral. The chances were, of course, that the police would accept Keble-Keith's death as suicide, but in matters of that sort one could never be a hundred-per-cent sure. Anyway, whatever happened, they would never suspect him. No one in the world knew that he had had a motive for killing Keble-Keith. No one, except perhaps that pallid young clerk who had handed him the rough stuff, but he didn't count. He probably hadn't even known Davidson's name, and in any case he would surely never connect the two incidents.

The day dragged aimlessly on, and when lunch-time came Lord Sanderlake had sandwiches and coffee sent up from the canteen. Soon after two o'clock the messenger who had gone to Keble-Keith's flat telephoned to say that he had been unable to get any answer. "I've knocked and rung any number of times without any result," he said, "but the people who live in the flat opposite say there's a daily woman who comes soon after three. Shall I wait around, my lord?"

"Yes, do that, would you? And keep in touch."

However, it was nearly half-past three before the messenger telephoned again, and by then Lord Sanderlake's face was shadowed by anxiety and nervous exhaustion. The afternoon editions of the *Evening Post* were spread out over his desk and they left no doubt as to the extent of his rival's success. Not an angle had been missed, and the front page carried huge photographs of Regan and Quince. 'The first beings from another planet ever to visit the Earth'. The middle pages were given over to accounts of Antigeos by Rose and Timothy Penn, and impressions of the Earth by Regan and Quince; and even Prue had been interviewed.

When the messenger came through he sounded excited. "Lord Sanderlake?" he gasped. "Bennett speaking. The daily woman let me into the flat, and when we went into the front room we found Mr. Keble-Keith lying there, dead! It looks as if he shot himself, and I called the police right away. They haven't arrived yet, and meantime I thought I'd better call you."

"Dead?" muttered Lord Sanderlake. "Good heavens! . . . Well, I must say you acted very sensibly. What did you say your name was?"

"Bennett, my lord."

"All right. We'll have to see if we can get you promoted to the reporting staff."

"Coo, thank you, sir—my lord, I mean."

Lord Sanderlake swung from the telephone to the dictograph and buzzed the news-editor.

"Preston? Send a man along to Mr. Keble-Keith's flat right away—you can get the address from Miss Nutt. It seems that he's shot himself. If so, it ties up with the spaceship story, of course, and it's front-page stuff."

"Very well, Lord Sanderlake."

"Oh, and, Preston—do you know the messenger Bennett? See if you can fit him in as a trainee reporter."

"Bennett? He's a bit young, isn't he?"

"Is he? Well, bear him in mind."

Lord Sanderlake had the impression that at last things were moving, and his mood changed to one of almost febrile cheerfulness. He grabbed the receiver from the telephone, and Davidson watched him apprehensively.

The newspaper-proprietor told the switchboard to get him No. 10 Downing Street. "I want to speak to Sir Willard Bute," he said, and Davidson's lip curled. He turned away with a hint of disgust and, going over to the wall of the office, gazed gloomily out through the glass. The sky was heavy with yellow fog, and although it was not yet four all the street-lamps were burning and the cars had their lights on. The weather matched Davidson's mood perfectly and, as he stared at the sepia sky, his impressions of an impending disaster intensified.

The telephone buzzed and Lord Sanderlake answered it. "Ah, Sir Willard? Sanderlake here. Look, I'm hoping you can arrange for me to have a talk with the Prime Minister. . . . Yes, I appreciate that, but I've just come by some rather significant news and I think he should hear of it. You see, this news is not unconnected with the spaceship's arrival. . . . Well, does the name Keble-Keith mean anything to you? . . . That's the man, and now I've just heard that he's shot himself.

. . . I was with him this morning and it struck me that he was in quite a state, but it never occurred to me that he, well, that he oughtn't to be left alone. . . . Well, I can hazard a guess. You see, it appears that he's been playing a very bent game, and this morning he actually admitted to me that ninety per cent of the information he'd been supplying me regarding Antigeos was fabricated. . . . I'm most grateful to you, Sir Willard. . . . Yes, I'll come along right away and if I have to wait—well, I'll have to wait, shan't I? . . . Good-bye."

Lord Sanderlake pushed the telephone from him and stood up. "All set, Davidson?" he asked. "We're going to Downing Street."

"Very well, my lord," muttered Davidson resignedly, and helped his master on with his overcoat.

Outside it was almost as dark as night. The traffic in the Strand crept along at a snail's pace and it took the Rolls-Royce nearly half an hour to get as far as Charing Cross. Lord Sanderlake sat biting his nails and once more became a prey to anxiety. "What's going on?" he muttered. "Surely the fog alone can't be responsible for this?"

"I couldn't say, my lord."

Lord Sanderlake noticed a policeman by the kerb, and wound down the window. "What's the hold-up, officer?"

The policeman recognised him and came forward. "We've been caught properly on the hop," he observed. "Whitehall's choked from top to bottom, and there must be a hundred thousand people in the Square. It's these here Antigeosians."

"What do you mean?"

"Why, a rumour's got about that they're going to see the Prime Minister. I don't think it's more than a rumour, mind you, but it's enough to draw the crowd.

Then the fog stopped the Arsenal–Everton match and all that lot's got down here."

The Rolls-Royce moved forward a few yards and the policeman disappeared. Lord Sanderlake could see Trafalgar Square now, and it was black with people. Many of the men wore football favours and the clatter of their rattles was deafening. People were singing lustily and Lord Sanderlake caught some words of the song, something about Regan and Quince and Antigeos, sung to the tune of a popular song. A man in a funny hat and playing a mouth-organ jumped on to the running-board of the Rolls-Royce and the crowd rallied round him, laughing and cheering.

Lord Sanderlake's nerves gave out, and, furious, he shouted to the man to get off, and in the next moment he was conscious of dozens of faces peering in at him, grinning and booing. Then suddenly the cry went up: "Cor, it's old Sanderlake!"

"Sanderlake? Where? Where?"

"Why, in the Rolls. Come on, let's chuck him in the fountain!"

It was said as a joke, but to Lord Sanderlake it seemed as if people were rushing towards him in waves, and he could feel himself sweating with terror.

A man yanked one of the doors of the car open, but the pressure of the crowd forced it shut again, and the newspaper-proprietor cowered into his corner, numb and cold with fear.

"It's old Sanderlake!" a woman screamed. "He tried to get us at war!"

The crowd surged as if in response to her cry, and the car was forced over the kerb. People were still trying to get the windows open, and others hammered on the windows with their fists. The Rolls lurched and rocked over the pavement, and Davidson blew the horn in one

185

unceasing blast. A few yards ahead were the portals of an office building, and now he saw in them a way of escape. He accelerated, pulling over closer to the wall and paying no attention to the curses and shrieks of the people at the front of the car. The car came abreast of the building's steps, and, throwing open the near-side door, he leapt out.

Lord Sanderlake had just enough sense left to open his own door and scramble from the car, and then the two of them raced up the steps and into the vestibule. Davidson spotted a lift and dragged his employer towards it, gaining it just as the first of the pursuers came storming into the building.

The lift shot upwards and Davidson turned to his white-faced, sweating employer. "If we can give them the slip for five minutes, we're saved," he muttered. "They're not seriously angry."

"They may not have been till you started running them down," snarled Lord Sanderlake. "Now if they catch us they'll lynch us."

"I didn't run anyone down. I caught one woman with my wing, and that's all."

The lift came to a stop at the top floor, and Davidson hauled the gates open. A mob of people were racing up the stairs and the whole building seemed to echo with the noise. A flight of stone steps led upwards towards a fire-door and the two fugitives pounded up them and emerged on to the roof. Electric sky-signs flashed and glimmered, and Davidson urged his master on towards the far end of the roof where there were a number of ventilation stacks separated from each other by gaps hardly eighteen inches wide.

Davidson caught Lord Sanderlake by the waist and thrust him towards one of the gaps. "Get in there!" he panted.

"I can't make it!" whimpered Lord Sanderlake, as Davidson pushed and shoved at him in an attempt to squeeze him in between the two concrete walls.

"You'll make it or get lynched!" gasped Davidson, then, barging the other as in a game of football, forced him into the gap.

Lord Sanderlake hit his head against the concrete and grazed his face on the ventilator's grilles, but he was in, and Davidson was following him.

"We've a chance," grunted Davidson. "No one'd ever think that you and me could get in here and——"

He broke off abruptly as, across the roof, the fire-door opened and their pursuers appeared. A dozen men burst out on to the roof and looked about them. In spite of the fog, the sky-signs and the bright lights of an electric newspaper illuminated the roof fairly well, and it took the would-be lynchers hardly a minute to decide there was no one up there.

"They must be hiding somewhere in the building!" shouted one. "Come on!"

The mob ran back towards the fire-exit, and met others in the doorway.

"No, there's no one up here," said the same voice as before. "You can look if you like, but you won't find anyone."

"Perhaps they've got away over the other roofs."

"Perhaps, but I doubt it. We were up here within a minute of the lift stopping."

Davidson peered through the ochreous gloom and tried to make out what was happening. People were still moving about in the vicinity of the fire-door and he whispered to Lord Sanderlake to get farther in. "My arm's showing," he breathed. "Squeeze yourself farther along, for God's sake!"

"I can't!" gasped Lord Sanderlake, but Davidson gave

him a violent shove and forced him farther along.

"Steady, Davidson!" he whispered. "You'll have me out at the other end!"

Davidson eased the pressure, and now through the far end of the gap Lord Sanderlake had a clear view of the electric newspapers and the sky-signs. Electric chorus-girls, twinkling and grinning, jerkily kicked their legs above their heads, and a gargantuan bottle, sparkling with green and yellow lights, poured an unending stream of golden brilliance into a glass half as tall as Nelson's Column; and between the two signs the harsh white lettering of the electric newspaper crept upwards into the darkness:

——RECEIVED PROF POLLENPORT AND A STATEMENT JUST ISSUED FROM 10 DOWN-ING ST ANNOUNCES THAT THE PRIME MINISTER WILL ADDRESS THE NATION AT 9–5 TONITE : : : : : GOVERNMENT CIRCLES ARE NOW FULLY CONVINCED THAT THE ANTIGEAN INTENTIONS ARE FRIENDLY AND AN INVITATION TO LAND IS BEING RADIOED TO THE SPACESHIP : : : : IT IS HOPED THAT THE SPACESHIP WILL LAND TOMORROW AND HYDE PARK HAS BEEN SUGGESTED AS A POSSIBLE LANDING GROUND BUT MUCH WILL DEPEND ON THE WEATHER : : : : THE CUP-TIE MATCH BETWEEN ARSENAL AND EVERTON DUE TO BE PLAYED AT WEMBLEY WAS POSTPONED OWING TO FOG AND TENS OF THOUSANDS OF DISAPPOINTED FANS HAVE INVADED WEST END IN HOPE OF SEEING PEOPLE FROM ANTIGEOS : : : : : THE ATTORNEY GENERAL SPEAKING TODAY AT PETERBORO

Davidson nudged Lord Sanderlake. "The roof's clear now," he whispered. "Let's get out of here!"

Lord Sanderlake edged his way painfully along the gap, then suddenly emerged and drew a deep breath of the grimy air. He felt numbed and defeated, and he no longer much cared what became of him. Beneath him, over to his right, he could see Trafalgar Square, packed with a dark mass of people, and Davidson clutched his sleeve. "Keep back!' he snapped. "They'll see you against those lights!"

Lord Sanderlake nodded dumbly and stumbled through the half-darkness in the general direction of the fire-door. Davidson hastily caught his arm. "Are you crazy?" he muttered. "We can't go down that way. They'll be waiting for us with ropes, and Christ knows what else."

He gazed about him wildly and saw that there was a cat-walk leading from the roof towards the sky-signs. It was an improvised affair of planks and tubular scaffolding, and no doubt normally it was used by the electricians who maintained the sky-signs.

"Come on," he said. "That'll take us to the next roof, and then we can think again. Only make it snappy, because we'll have the lights behind us."

Lord Sanderlake gazed at the cat-walk and recoiled. "I couldn't!" he gasped. "I've got no head for heights."

"Then what the hell are you doing up here? Come on!"

Davidson urged him forward, and Lord Sanderlake

no longer had the will-power to resist. His hand gripped the rail of tubular scaffolding and he stepped up on to the plank, moving gingerly forward with Davidson at his back. Then, half-way across, he suddenly looked down in horror at the sixty-foot drop and every muscle went tense.

"Go on!" cried Davidson. "We're dead against the light!"

He tried to push his master forward and Lord Sanderlake screamed, and in the next moment there came a great roar of sound from the Square.

"You bloody fool, they've seen us," muttered Davidson. "Go on!"

And from beneath them a hundred thousand people watched them silhouetted against the sky-signs and struggling desperately as Davidson tried to break Lord Sanderlake's grip on the rail. He brought his fist down on to the other's arm and in the same moment tried to lift him bodily with his other arm about him. Then his foot slipped on the greasy plank and, off-balance, he clutched wildly at the rail, letting go of Lord Sanderlake.

The newspaper-proprietor clawed the air for a second, then fell backwards into the darkness. A power-cable broke his fall, and briefly Davidson glimpsed him swinging there, hardly four feet below him, then the cable snapped and Lord Sanderlake hurtled to his death with a shriek of terror that a hundred thousand people would never forget.

Half the lights of the electric newspaper went out, and the snapped cable came snaking back through the darkness like a live thing. It's naked end scattered great flashes of blue lightning along the cat-walk, and as the voltage struck Davidson he jerked convulsively against the rail, losing consciousness at once and dying within the minute. Then somewhere a fuse blew and the power-cable fell away to dangle harmlessly against the wall, while Davidson's body slid down to the planks of the cat-walk and balanced there precariously, sixty feet above the street. . . .

VII

The giant spaceship was coming in to land and all Sam Spencross could think of was what a mug he'd look, walking about Hyde Park in an Antigean tunic.

"No, I'm not fooling," he said, with immense seriousness. "I'm not going to put my nose outside this contraption until someone turns up with a respectable suit."

"S-sh, listen!" exclaimed Paul. "That's music, isn't it?"

They were in the radio-room, and Paul's gaze was fixed on one of the amplifiers. They were now below the Heaviside-Kennelly layer, just below it, and at any moment they expected to start picking up normal radio programmes.

The amplifier hissed and crackled, and somewhere behind the atmospherics Paul was sure he could hear the throb of music. He touched a dial and then there was no doubt about it. "Sam, a military band!" he exclaimed. "Gee, they assure us we shall not be met with hostilities and what do we get? *Colonel Bogey!*"

He touched the dial again, the music grew louder and with it came the sound of an announcer's voice: ". . . the scene here in Hyde Park is absolutely dazzling and there's simply no other word for it. The sun is

shining and the birds are singing and all that part of
the Park where the spaceship will land is just a vast
expanse of green. Actually, the crowds are being
extraordinarily good, very well disciplined indeed—
don't you think so, Richard—and the police are doing
a wonderful job, too. . . . I expect you heard that
terrific cheer that just went up? Pollenport and his party
have arrived! They're just getting out of their car
and through my glasses I can distinguish Professor
Pollenport—yes, and Quince—Regan—oh yes—Rose
and Timothy Penn, and, of course, Prue. She's walking
between her parents in a very pretty blue dress, and
an official is escorting them all towards the Royal
Stand. . . ."

A certain amount of muttering interrupted the com-
mentary at that point and then the announcer came
on again: "I've just been told that the spaceship is now
estimated to be below the Heaviside layer, which, of
course, means that the people on the spaceship are probably picking up this broadcast. Our engineers are
hoping to make contact with them within the next few
minutes and if they're successful no doubt Sam Spencross and Paul Greenwood will speak to you and tell
you what all this is like from their angle. . . ."

"Oh Gawd," muttered Sam. "I'm no good at that
sort of caper."

Paul laughed and turned down the volume. He
moved to the other receiving set, on which he was hoping
to pick up the B.B.C.'s technical staff. He switched on
and, tuning in, almost immediately picked up the transmission: "Hullo, this is B.B.C. 34 calling Antigean
spaceship. Are you getting us? This is B.B.C. 34 calling . . ."

Paul leant over to the transmission-unit and pulled
the microphone towards him. "B.B.C. 34? This is the

spaceship, Paul Greenwood speaking. Yes, we're getting both you and the outside broadcast, and the reception's excellent."

"Fine," said the B.B.C. man. "And now we'd like to put you out on the programme. Would you and Sam Spencross say a few words?"

Sam nudged Paul violently. "Tell him no," he whispered.

Paul laughed again and turned back to the microphone. "Sam seems a little reluctant," he said, "but I guess we'll do our best."

"Good. Stand by."

A minute later word came back that they were on the air, and Paul took it upon himself to greet the people of Britain on behalf of all on board the spaceship. "I guess that's a little impertinent of me," he said, "but none of the Antigeosians are in the radio-compartment, and I cannot get Sam Spencross to speak. Now come on, Sam—say Hullo."

Sam blushed violently and drew a deep breath. "Hullo, everybody," he said. "This is Sam Spencross—er-um—well, I mean—er-um—there's not much I want to say, except that it's grand to be home again and—um—well, I'm looking forward to smoking a pipe of tobacco again. You see, I haven't had a smoke for five years and, well, I'm looking forward to one. Er-um—I think everything on the spaceship is in good order for the landing. I was in the control-compartment less than five minutes ago and—um—the engineers assured me that everything is favourable for a perfect landing. Of course, so far we're still using jet units to break our fall—and, I believe, the big reactors—but by the time we're visible to the people in Hyde Park we shall, of course, be coming down on the helicopter units. . . ."

Fifty miles beneath them Prue wriggled and fidgeted

between Timothy and Rose. "What are we waiting for, Mummy?" she asked.

"The spaceship."

"I know, but what else?"

Rose laughed. "Don't you want to see Sam and Paul?"

"Yes," said Prue, without excitement. "But I do want to see the animals' place."

"What? Oh, the Zoo. Well, we'll take you there soon."

"Today?"

"No, not today," said Rose, and at that moment Prue's attention was distracted by two mounted police-men cantering by.

"Mummy, *look*!" she screamed.

Rose was mystified until Prue pointed and then, with a slight feeling of guilt, it occurred to her that, although she had told Prue about most terrestrial animals, horses had been rather neglected. "Those are called horses," she explained. "They're a sort of animal."

"Are they like lions?"

"Well, no," said Rose, smiling. "Horses and lions are both animals, but apart from that they're not much alike."

"Well, are they like tigers?"

"Not a bit."

"Or are they like elephants?"

"Not much," said Rose. "Oh, Timothy, you explain."

"Well——" began Timothy, but at that moment the two policemen came cantering back and Prue fastened her attention upon them to the exclusion of all else.

She watched them seriously until they were out of sight, and then announced that the top part of them looked like people. "With faces," she said. "Like people with faces."